THE CLOUD HORSE CHRONICLES
Guardians of Magic

Other books from Chris Riddell

CHRIS RIDDELL

THE CLOUD HORSE CHRONICLES

Guardians of Magic

MACMILLAN CHILDREN'S BOOKS

First published 2019 by Macmillan Children's Books
an imprint of Pan Macmillan
The Smithson, 6 Briset Street, London EC1M 5NR
Associated companies throughout the world
www.panmacmillan.com

ISBN 978-1-4472-7797-2

1 3 5 7 9 8 6 4 2

A CIP catalogue record for this book is available from
the British Library.

Typeset by Viki Ottewill and Sue Mason
Printed and bound in Poland by Dimograf

For Stephen

THRYNNE

Fairy tales don't behave in the land of Thrynne. Not any more.

Magic was once something precious for everyone. And the magic of nature and its source, the Forever Tree, was prized above all else, because that magic made people creative, sensitive and brave.

But three enemies are working together to destroy the power of the Forever Tree. If they succeed, soon its magic will be gone and so will the cloud horses that nestle in its branches.

Who are these enemies?

The King Rat and his followers from the city of Troutwine fear magic. It could return them to their forest roots, and now they crave only the pleasures the city has to offer.

The Clockmaker of the city of Nightingale wants to control magic, using his mechanical inventions to keep power for himself alone.

And the Professional Princess with her crew of giant-slayers from the town of Beam is happy to work with both of them, if it brings her the fame and fortune she craves.

But in the heart of the Forever Tree, magical gifts are being prepared for three children who don't yet know how powerful they are . . .

In the depths of the Great Wood stands the Forever Tree. It is huge. The bark on its trunk is gnarled and grooved with paw-holds. Dark-furred bears, known as the lumberers, carefully prune and bundle the smaller branches, then carry them on their backs down to the forest floor.

A light shines from a nook deep in the tangle of roots, and the lumberers step into a tree-root workshop, laying the bundles of Forever wood on a bench. An old lady with silvery hair sorts the branches carefully into shapes and sizes she can use.

Then she turns to the tools racked on the walls and selects the ones she needs for the job.

The lumberers turn and leave as the sounds of sawing, planing and sanding start. The sounds last far into the night; the workshop's lights glint in the dark.

As dawn rises, the old lady emerges. A wagon driven by lumberers pulls up. It is covered in oilcloth. The words 'The Ursine Ballet Troupe of the West' are painted on its side. The old lady reaches into her apron pocket and takes out a glowing slotted spoon with a long handle, which she hands to one of the bears.

'For Zam Zephyr at Bakery No. 9, Troutwine,' she says and returns to her workshop. Hanging from a hook are the front and back panels of a very special cello, destined for Phoebe Limetree, a young musician in the city of Nightingale. On the workbench, clamped in a vice, is the handle of a worpal sword for Bathsheba Greengrass, a giant-slayer's daughter from the town of Beam.

The old lady dims the lamp and turns to find a bear holding out a bowl of porridge. She takes it, then takes the bear's arm, and they leave the workshop. 'It starts tomorrow,' she says.

High above the workshop, in the uppermost branches of the Forever Tree, is a nest of glowing twigs, woven together and lined with glittering moss. In the nest are eggs as white as the whitest cloud, dotted with speckles of sky blue. The eggs are stirring, hatching. Tiny lines criss-cross their surfaces, growing wider with each tremor and twitch . . .

Before long, a shadow falls over the leaves, and another, and there is a whooshing sound as two flying horses swoop down from the sky. Beneath them, in the tree branches, nestled in the moss, are three newly hatched tiny winged foals.

For as long as anyone can remember, the children of Thrynne have looked at billowing clouds in the sky and wished on a cloud horse, always hoping, but never quite believing, that their wish will come true. No one has ever seen a cloud horse. But that is about to change . . .

1

1

THE RUNCIBLE SPOON

Zam Zephyr woke early and climbed out of bed, careful not to disturb the other apprentice bakers of Bakery No. 9, who were still fast asleep around him.

It was the day before the Grand Duchess of Troutwine's Tea Ball and Zam was too excited and nervous to stay in bed. Today, they would bake for the tea ball tomorrow. All twelve bakeries in the city competed for the honour of making the most delicious treats for the ball. If anything went wrong again, after last year's disaster that put Bakery No. 9 at the bottom of the heap, Zam and his friends would be sent home in disgrace. The thought of his father's disappointed face was too much to bear. No, Zam thought. He would do anything he could to make sure that his baking was perfect.

In the corner of the attic dormitory, his best friend Langdale the goat boy was gently snoring. Beneath the flour-sack blanket, his hooves twitched as he dreamed of chasing blue butterflies through the summer pine forests of the Western Mountains. In the other corner, the two Shellac sisters clutched the comfort shawl they shared. In the cots in between, the gnome boys from the Grey Hills slept soundless and still, five to a blanket, their small grey-tufted heads just visible.

Looking out of the window, Zam could see the golden roofs of the palaces glittering in the early morning sunlight. He gazed up at a billowing cloud and made a wish: 'To bake the best gingerbread ever,' he whispered. 'Cloud horse, cloud horse, far from view, make this wish of mine come true.'

Zam took his apron and cap from the hook and crept out of the attic, leaving his friends to their dreams.

Zam ran all the way down the stairs to the

basement, opened the door to the flavour library, and stepped inside. This was his favourite place. He loved how precise, tidy and ordered everything was here. He smiled to himself. With everyone asleep upstairs, it was the perfect time of day to practise without any interruptions.

Shelves lined the basement walls from floor to vaulted ceiling. Looking up through the glass paving stone, Zam could see the shadows of feet walking overhead as people passed the doors of Bakery No. 9.

The shelves around him were stacked with jars of all shapes and sizes, each clearly labelled.

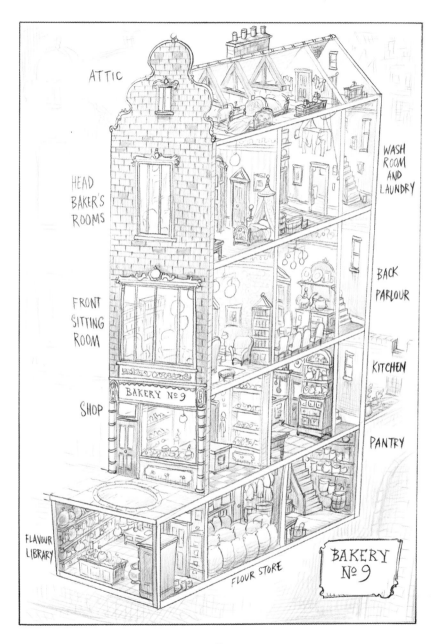

ATTIC

HEAD
BAKER'S
ROOMS

FRONT
SITTING
ROOM

SHOP

BAKERY Nº 9

WASH
ROOM
AND
LAUNDRY

BACK
PARLOUR

KITCHEN

PANTRY

FLAVOUR
LIBRARY

FLOUR STORE

BAKERY
Nº 9

8

Zam selected the jars he needed, opening each one in turn and taking pinches of the powders they contained.

Carefully, he placed the spices on little squares of baking parchment, which he folded neatly and placed in different pockets of his apron. Satisfied with his choices, Zam crossed the stone floor to a large chest of drawers set in an alcove. He opened a drawer labelled 'Index of Crusts' and selected one with crinkle-cut edges and memorized the baking instructions written in small lettering on the underside.

'*For a crumbly texture, short, intense mixing and slow bake in quiet oven . . .*' Zam read. The memory of the calm, reassuring sound of the head baker's voice filled his head, as it always did when Zam read his recipes. '*For a more robust biscuit, easeful mixing with broad, generous spoon and a short, fierce bake in busy oven . . .*'

'Broad, generous spoon,' Zam repeated to himself, returning the crinkle-cut crust to the drawer and closing it. He looked up and was about to select one of the wooden spoons, which hung from the hooks in the ceiling, when he trod on something. It was a large spoon he hadn't noticed lying on the flagstone floor.

'That is so careless,' Zam muttered, picking it up. The spoon was broad and long handled, carved from a single piece of wood, by the look of it. Zam turned it over. It was a slotted spoon, full of small holes, with three large ones near the base of the handle.

'Easeful mixing with broad, generous spoon,' the head baker's voice sounded in Zam's head.

'Perfect,' he said, wiping the spoon

on his apron before slipping it into a pocket.

He selected a favourite battered old book from a shelf: *The Art of Baking*. 'There you are,' he said happily and climbed the back stairs to the kitchen.

An hour later, the other apprentice bakers had been woken by the six o'clock gong and were filing in, putting on their caps and rubbing the sleep from their eyes. Balthazar Boabab, the head baker of Bakery No. 9, followed them into the kitchen smiling.

'Good morning, apprentices!' he said cheerfully, peering over the top of his half-rim spectacles. 'As you know, the twelve bakeries of

Troutwine are baking for the Grand Duchess's Tea Ball tomorrow, and we all have our parts to play.'

The head baker smiled again, a little ruefully this time. 'Bakery No. 1 is doing the first tiers. Bakery No. 2 the second and third tiers. Fillings are being produced by bakeries No. 3, 4 and 5. While No. 6, 7 and 8 are baking pastry shells and meringues. Bakeries No. 10 and 11 are fruitcake and turnovers, and Bakery No. 12 is making floating islands . . .'

Balthazar Boabab took

a deep breath. 'This means, once again, Bakery No. 9 is picking up the crumbs . . .'

The apprentice bakers began to mutter. It wasn't fair. They had tried so hard, but they weren't being given a chance.

'I know, I know . . .' said the head baker. 'It's not ideal, but after last year's cake collapse and exploding-eclair incident, Bakery No. 9 has a lot to prove . . .'

'But that wasn't our fault,' protested one of the gnomes.

'The last head baker didn't pay off the League of Rats,' said Langdale the goat boy, stamping his hooves, 'and they ruined everything . . .'

'Nothing was proved,' said Balthazar gently. 'I am head baker now, and things are different, aren't they?'

Zam and the other apprentices nodded. It was true. Bakery No. 9 had changed since Balthazar Boabab had taken over: no more bullying, tantrums or random punishments. The kitchen was a happy place, and everyone was respected and baking beautifully. It was just as well. A year ago, after the disaster of the last tea ball, Bakery No. 9 had almost been shut down and everyone sent home. If Balthazar hadn't joined them from the fashionable Bakery No. 12, the apprentices would have had no future. None of them wanted to let him down.

'But what about the rats?' asked Langdale anxiously.

'Let me worry about them,' said the head baker, doing his best to sound cheerful. 'After all, we have heard nothing from the rats since I arrived.

'Meanwhile, you have baking to do. We will be making the crusts as well as gingerbread and some spun-sugar decorations. And, at the tea ball itself –'

Balthazar cleared his throat; even he couldn't sound cheerful about the next bit – 'Bakery No. 9 will be doing the washing-up.'

The apprentice bakers groaned.

'Langdale and the Shellac sisters are on shortcrust pastry shells,' Balthazar instructed. 'Gnomes are on glazed piecrust. Zam, are you confident to bake the gingerbread and help me with the spun sugar?'

'Yes, head baker,' said Zam excitedly. 'I've already been down in the flavour library . . .'

'Baker's pet,' muttered Langdale.

Balthazar gave the goat boy a stern look. But before he could say anything, an unexpected sound silenced them all.

In the shop, the doorbell had rung, and now they could hear the scritch-scratch of claws on the floorboards.

'I smell a rat,' said Langdale.

16

2

THE SUGAR-SPUN PRINCESS

The rat was the size of a small cat, which was not uncommon for the rats of Troutwine. For as long as most people could remember, the town had been plagued by rats. Each generation seemed to grow bigger and more sophisticated. These days, the Troutwine rats wore jackets and fancy waistcoats made specially for them. They carried catapults and swag bags ready for anything they could lay their paws on.

They lurked in the shadows, gutters and sewers, but less often than they used to. Now they could be seen in small groups walking about on the streets quite openly.

The rats had even started shaving the tops and sides of their heads in imitation of the townsfolk. This rat was no different.

Zam peered carefully round the door. The rat had a fuzzy layer of stubble on his head and cheeks, and the fur remaining was combed into braids from which small silver spoons hung. He had a catapult in the back pocket of his jacket and a bundle of large matches for starting fires poking out of his swag bag.

Balthazar Boabab strode past Zam and into the shop. 'Can I help you?' he said politely. 'But before I do, can I just say what a magnificent waistcoat that is; it suits you so well—'

'So, you're the new head baker, are you?' interrupted the rat, his whiskers quivering as he sniffed the air. 'We heard they got rid of old Wilkins.'

'Balthazar Boabab. Very pleased to meet you – though I'm not so new. Head baker Wilkins left just about a year ago . . .' Balthazar explained. 'Can I just say, I love what you've done with your hair.'

'Well, thank you very much,' said the rat, swelling

with pride. 'Walters-Walters is the name. Been leaving Bakery No. 9 alone for a while since last year's little trouble, haven't we. But now you're back on your feet, we want a taste.'

'A taste?' said Balthazar innocently.

'Half your money every week, starting right now,' said Walters-Walters. 'Or your luck will change: fires might start; windows might get broken; people might slip on greasy flagstones . . .'

'I see,' said Balthazar, crossing to the counter and scooping five crescent-shaped bread rolls on to a square of greased parchment and folding it neatly.

'I wish I could oblige you. I really do,' he said. 'But I'm sure that an intelligent and fashionable gentleman such as yourself will understand that we have spent this week's takings on supplies for the Grand Duchess's Tea Ball tomorrow. Perhaps you'll accept these for now . . . ?' Balthazar deftly slipped the package of delicious buttery rolls into the rat's swag bag.

Walters-Walters paused for a moment, eyeing the mouth-watering gift and considering Balthazar's suggestion. 'I wouldn't normally do this, but I like you. I don't know why, but I do. So, I'll give you till the end of the week.'

The rat turned, opening the bakery door so that the bell attached to it wouldn't ring, slipped through the narrow gap sleekly and silently, and was gone.

Balthazar slumped against the counter for a moment, looking suddenly very tired. He caught Zam watching from the doorway that led down to the kitchen and straightened up, attempting to smile.

'Don't look so worried, Zam,' he said brightly. 'I'll take care of it. Now, haven't you got some gingerbread to make?'

*

Zam looked down at the ingredients in the bowl. He had to get this just right. He would blame himself if everything wasn't perfect.

Taking the wooden spoon, he began to stir the flour and all the spices he'd selected so carefully from the flavour library, together with eggs and golden syrup. The spoon slid around the bowl effortlessly and seemed to glow and grow warm in Zam's hands. He muttered the recipe: '*Easeful mixing with broad, generous spoon.*'

He had the baking tray ready. It was the biggest one in the kitchen, and he'd had to persuade Langdale to let him use it. The others had all finished their tasks by now, and they were upstairs having tea with the head baker. This was one of Balthazar's ideas. It brought everyone together during the busy day. Zam would have his cup of tear-water tea later, once he'd got the gingerbread with crinkle-cut edges safely in the oven.

Zam spooned the mixture from the bowl on to the baking tray and then carried it across to the enormous oven. He pulled on the heavy gloves before opening the door and quickly placed the tray inside as a fiery blast hit him. Zam pushed the door closed, his heart beating fast. '*Short, fierce bake . . .*' he reminded himself. The oven was fierce all right, and it was busy too. Its other shelves were crammed with Langdale and the Shellac sisters' shortcrust shells.

Zam was just about to go upstairs and join the others when he noticed something on the head baker's table. It was a porcelain cake decorator's dummy and a pan full of sugar and water. Zam smiled. He loved working with sugar but hadn't had much practice so far. It wouldn't do any harm to have a go.

He took the pan over to the stove, added a splash of rosewater, and heated it, stirring all the time with the wooden spoon. The sugar dissolved and

turned a beautiful golden colour. Zam took the pan over to the cake decorator's dummy and scooped up the golden mixture and spun it round and round the dummy. As he worked, the spoon glowed and became warmer and warmer in his hand. It felt as if it had a life of its own.

A few moments later, Zam stepped back from the table and gasped. There, cooling on the porcelain dummy, was a sugar-spun princess. Zam looked down at the spoon thoughtfully, turning it over in his hand. It seemed to be perfectly clean with no trace of the sticky sugar mixture. It was almost as if the spoon was . . . 'Magical.' Zam trembled as he breathed the word.

Magical objects and their use were forbidden in Troutwine. The rats hated magic, and the people of Troutwine avoided upsetting the rats if they knew what was good for them. Perhaps it wasn't magical, Zam thought to himself. Perhaps his sugar work had just improved . . .

Pushing his worries to the back of his mind,
Zam put the spoon in his apron pocket and
climbed the stairs. He was looking forward to
that cup of tea while the gingerbread baked.

3

TEAR-WATER TEA

Zam took a sip of his tea. It tasted a little salty, but tear-water tea was always very good. If you were lonely or homesick, it was said that the taste of tear-water tea would make you feel better.

In the back parlour, the apprentice bakers sat back contentedly in the cake-tin chairs.

'Good morning's work, everyone,' said Balthazar, glancing at the grandfather clock in the corner and refilling their cups from an enormous teapot. 'The ovens are full, the piecrusts are cooking, and it's almost nine o'clock.'

'Opening time,' yawned Langdale, who had his feet up and arms behind his head.

'Hooves off the furniture,' said Balthazar. He put the teapot down on the sideboard beside the chimney. 'Now, everyone drink up. Then it's down to the shop for uniform inspection.'

Zam was just getting to his feet when Balthazar spotted him. 'You had an extra early start,' the head baker said peering down at him kindly through his half-rim spectacles, which were now lightly dusted with flour. 'Take a little more time to finish your tea.'

Zam sat back down as the other apprentice bakers filed out of the back parlour. The gnome boys adjusted their caps, the Shellac sisters checked the buttons on each other's jackets, and Langdale stuck out his tongue at Zam, then giggled as Zam did the same.

The boy took another sip of the lightly salted tea and let his mind wander. His thoughts went back to his family and his childhood home on the Sea of Sand. In his mind, he could see the great caravan winding its way across the dunes, the sails of the sandwalkers billowing as they pulled the sand sleighs on thousands of rippling wooden legs. His father was out in front, as he always was, charting their course, his blue robes bright against the white sand. Zam sat beside his mother in the cool shade of a cabin, the smell of warm, sweet dates mingling with the aroma of see spice and rock salt, until a call from his father sent him running across the hot sand, beside the huge wooden sandwalker with its cogs and pulleys. He adjusted the little lead weights, pulling the levers to angle the rows of sails to catch the desert breeze.

And then his memory took Zam back to Troutwine's North River Bridge, where he stood in his crisp white apron and a new cap that was a little too big for him. Fighting back the tears after saying goodbye to his parents, he struggled not to lose sight of his father's blue robes in the far distance. His mother's words rang in his head: *'Work hard, Zam, and make us proud.'*

Zam finished the tear-water tea and wiped his eyes. 'I will work hard,' he said, feeling a little better. 'I will make you proud.'

He went down the back stairs to the kitchen to join his friends, only to find everyone gathered around the head baker's table. Balthazar Boabab turned to Zam, his eyes wide with astonishment.

'This is excellent work, Zam!' he congratulated, pointing to the sugar-spun princess cooling on the porcelain cake decorator's dummy. 'I had no idea you had such a talent for spun-sugar work.'

'Neither did I,' said Zam, blushing.

'Can I lick the saucepan?' interrupted Langdale, who was holding the pan under his arm.

'Certainly not!' said Balthazar sternly. 'You can wash it up, like a true baker, and then join us for inspection.'

The goat boy went off sulkily to the stone sink as the others marched upstairs into the shop. They lined up in front of the counter while Balthazar checked their jackets and caps for neatness and jam stains.

'Excellent,' he said when he'd finished. 'Except for you, Langdale.' He turned to the goat boy who had just joined his friends. 'You appear to have caramel on your side whiskers.'

Langdale tried to look innocent as he wiped his mouth with the corner of his apron.

'Never mind,' said Balthazar. 'It's time to open Bakery No. 9.'

The Shellac sisters walked over to the door and turned the sign hanging from it to 'Open', while the others took their positions around the shop.

The gnome boys were ready to pluck pastries and tarts from the shelves, while the Shellac sisters folded purchases into neat greased-parchment parcels and tied them with string. Langdale and Zam were on tray filling, ready to replenish the shop shelves with fresh cakes, pastries and biscuits from the kitchen. Balthazar stood by the coin box on the counter.

The doorbell rang as the first customers entered. They had been waiting patiently outside for ten minutes in order to get the freshest just-baked

bread. There were two lamp lighters, a group of
fish sellers and several well-dressed ladies from
the 'high-ups', as the most expensive districts at
the top of the Troutwine crags were called. They
had footmen with them. The customers gave their
orders, the apprentices served them, and the head
baker collected the coins.

'Twenty-four crescent rolls, my good man,' said one of the 'high-up' ladies in a loud voice. The crescent rolls were popular, and already there were only ten left on the shelves.

Balthazar nodded to Zam to get a fresh batch. He could also check on the oven while he was there.

Zam hurried down to the kitchen but was shocked

to find two rats staring back at him. Each was holding a crescent roll, which they hastily put into their swag bags.

'No customers allowed in the kitchen!' said Zam, trying to sound confident.

'Oh, we're not customers,' said the first rat, who had a shaved head and rings in its ears.

'We're friends of Walters-Walters,' said the second rat, who was smaller than the first and had dark, greasy fur. 'He said you were giving away free crescent rolls . . .'

'Well, we're not!' said Zam indignantly, trying to appear brave. He hated how high-pitched his voice sounded.

The rats' eyes suddenly widened, and they exchanged astonished looks.

'Can you see what I see, Rufus-Rufus?' said the greasy-looking rat.

'I can, Erics-Erics,' said the rat with the shaved head.

They were staring at Zam's apron pocket where

the carved handle of the spoon was clearly visible.

'It is, ain't it . . . ?' said the greasy rat.

'A runcible spoon!' said the other.

Just then, the door to the oven burst open with a deafening crash, and baking trays and shortcrust shells flew out in all directions.

4

GINGER

Zam ducked, and as he threw himself to the floor to avoid a flying baking tray, he felt the greasy fur of a rat brush past his raised hands. There was a series of deafening crashes as the trays landed in various parts of the kitchen together with a shower of crumbs and billows of smoke and steam.

When Zam looked up, the rats had gone, but the kitchen was a mess. The trays from the exploding oven had knocked over the cooling shelves, scattering rolls and pastries everywhere. A flour sack had split, and a milk churn had been overturned, and the resulting mixture was slowly spreading across the flagstone floor.

Shattered shortcrust pastry shells lay in gently smoking heaps, and slumped over the lip of the open oven was a great mass of gingerbread. The only object unaffected by the explosion seemed to be the sugar-spun princess, which had somehow ended up on its own two elegant feet in the far corner of the kitchen. The porcelain cake decorator's dummy, meanwhile, had smashed to pieces on the floor.

Zam was just puzzling over this when he felt a hand on his shoulder.

'Zam, are you all right?' It was Balthazar. Together with the apprentices and a couple of customers, he was looking down at Zam with concern.

'I think so,' said Zam, getting to his feet and brushing pastry crumbs out of his hair.

'I found two rats in the kitchen . . .' he began, but Balthazar quickly silenced him with a look and took him to one side.

'Not so loud,' the head baker whispered. He turned to the others. 'Everybody back to the shop,' he instructed cheerfully. 'It's nothing to worry about. Accidents will happen.'

Once the kitchen was clear, Balthazar took Zam gently by the arm. 'Don't mention the rats,' he cautioned. 'If word got out they were in our bakery, it could ruin us. I'll find the money to pay them off somehow. Just thought I had more time . . .'

Zam could hear loud voices in the shop. 'Where are my crescent rolls and what was that awful crashing sound?'

'You clear up the kitchen, Zam, there's a good lad, while I smooth things over with the customers. I'll send Langdale in to give you a hand.'

The head baker hurried back to the shop.

Zam looked around for the broom.

'They stole it,' said a small, sweet voice.

'The broom?' said Zam confused, trying to work out who had spoken.

'No, the spoon, silly.' The voice gave a little tinkling laugh. 'I saw the rats take it from your pocket when the mountain of gingerbread burst out of the oven.'

Zam swallowed hard, then rubbed his eyes. It couldn't be . . . could it?

The sugar-spun princess stepped daintily out of the corner and tiptoed across the floor, avoiding the milky sludge as she did so.

'You're . . . You're alive!' Zam gasped.

'Of course,' she said. 'You made me with a runcible spoon. Just like you made Ginger . . .'

Zam followed the sugar-spun princess's gaze. As he watched, the mass of gingerbread rippled and flexed, then gathered itself up on to what Zam could only describe as its feet. It must have expanded in the heat of the oven, because now it towered over Zam.

The sugar-spun princess danced across the kitchen, gathering up spoons, forks and spatulas, which she took over to the gingerbread. It held out two great arms, and she pressed the cutlery into the ends until it had an impressive array of 'fingers'.

'Runcible spoon?' Zam's head was still spinning.

'Yes. The spoon that made me,' said the sugar-spun princess. 'It was carved from the wood of the Forever Tree,' she continued. 'And it must be full of magic, otherwise I wouldn't be able to talk, or think, or do this.'

She danced around the kitchen while Ginger clapped his hands together, making the spoons and forks clank and clink.

'What the . . . ?'

Zam turned to see that Langdale had trotted into the kitchen and was staring at the living mountain of gingerbread.

As the goat boy fainted, Ginger caught Langdale gently in his arms and laid him down on the split flour sack.

Ginger turned to the sugar-spun princess and swayed from side to side, stamping his feet. A shower of crumbs tumbled down as a split appeared in the shape of a smile in his lumpy face. Two dark eyeholes opened above the mouth. Ginger blinked, then opened his mouth, and a rumbling sound rose up from deep within. It sounded like bubbling toffee and pudding bowls being scraped. The sugar-spun princess stopped dancing and craned her neck upwards, head to one side, listening. She turned to Zam.

'Ginger says that the runcible spoon is calling to him,' she explained.

'Calling to him?' Zam said, looking up at Ginger's crumbly face staring back at him. It certainly was powerful magic, and Zam had caused all of this by using that strange spoon. He knew magic was not allowed, and a powerful object like that could spell trouble for Bakery No. 9, but despite everything, Zam felt a shiver of excitement run through him. 'What's the runcible spoon saying?' he asked.

5

THE WATER BADGER

Zam followed Ginger and the princess out of the
back door of the kitchen. They lumbered across the
tiny courtyard outside. Leaning forward from her
perch on Ginger's shoulder, the sugar-spun princess
slipped the latch on the gate.

Ginger stepped into the narrow alley behind
Bakery No. 9, and the princess raised a sugary hand
to shield her eyes from the morning sunshine.
Above the three of them, white sheets on the
washing lines that criss-crossed the alley billowed
like the sales of a vast ship.

The sugar-spun princess tapped Ginger on his
shoulder. 'Which way?' she whispered.

He lowered his huge head, his forehead
wrinkling above his cake-hole eyes, then he opened
his mouth. A rumbling rattling sound, like biscuits

trapped in a tin, rose up from the depths of his body. The sugar-spun princess nodded.

'What did he say?' asked Zam.

She pointed to a circular iron grille set into the cobblestones. 'He says the runcible spoon is down there.'

'The sewers!' exclaimed Zam with a shudder. He looked up into the large glazed eyes of the sugar-spun princess and then at Ginger. They both seemed so alive, and they trusted him, Zam realized. Whatever strange magic the runcible spoon possessed, it was powerful. With the spoon, Zam had stirred and spun life into these two extraordinary creations: the heavy, hard-baked Ginger; and the delicate, quick-witted princess. Just imagine what else he could make using the runcible spoon. Zam didn't even want to think what the rats might do with it. He had to get it back . . .

Ginger gave a crumbly, syrupy groan.

'Are you coming with us?' asked the sugar-spun

princess. 'Only, Ginger says we don't have much time.'

The townsfolk of Troutwine avoided the sewers beneath their city. They stepped over the grilles that covered the tunnel entrances as if they weren't there. And if one centimetre opened, and a rat slipped out, the townsfolk would look the other way. The sewers' channels, vaults and chambers were ancient, dark and mysterious, and the townsfolk didn't want to know what went on down there. They paid the League of Rats handsomely to keep it that way.

'Yes,' said Zam, swallowing hard. 'I'm coming with you.'

Beneath the grille, circular stone steps led down into darkness. Zam followed Ginger and the princess, pulling the grille back into place behind him. Instead of pitch black, Zam could see the steps as they descended, and he realized that the sugar-spun princess was glowing faintly.

She glanced back at him and gave a reassuring

smile. At the bottom of the steps was a low, arched tunnel with a channel full of water flowing through it and a walkway alongside. Nervously avoiding the water, they made their way carefully along the walkway, past the openings to other smaller tunnels, then down more steps into high-vaulted chambers that echoed with the scritch-scratch of claws.

Zam glanced around. Despite the sounds, he could see no rats anywhere. Just then, a strange raft came floating around the corner towards them on the flowing water. A figure stooped over a long-handled paddle, propelling the collection of wooden boards, broken furniture and crates that made up the vessel. The figure looked up, pushing the brim of its hat back to reveal a white snout and two black patches of fur around its eyes.

Zam gasped. 'A water badger.'

'That's right, young sir,' said the water badger. 'And you're going the wrong way if you don't want to run into big trouble.'

Before Zam could answer, the badger's nose wrinkled as he sniffed the air. 'Ah . . . gingerbread! And . . . something sweet . . .' He turned his gaze from Zam to Ginger and the glowing princess.

'So, the rat gossip is true,' the badger said. 'Tree magic, by the look of you two.' He nodded towards Ginger and the princess.

'Please help us,' said Zam. 'We're looking for a runcible spoon. The rats stole it, and we have to get it back.'

The water badger shook his head and turned away, but before he left, he said, 'The rats are all in the main chamber upstream. I would hurry if I were you – they're planning to burn that spoon they stole.'

The raft disappeared into the darkness, taking the badger with it.

'You heard him!' said the princess. 'We've got to hurry. If they burn the spoon, that'll be the end of its magic, and the end of Ginger and me!'

Further up the tunnel, the sound of scritch-scratching grew louder, and Zam could hear raised voices.

'Down with tree magic! Burn the spoon! Burn the spoon.'

6

KING RAT & THE GRAND DUCHESS

Zam crept towards the corner of the sewer and
peered round it. He saw a large chamber full of other
sewer openings, and next to them, stone balconies
packed to bursting with expensively clothed rats.

Below, on a raised platform in the middle of a
large pool, was a rusty-looking iron brazier, around
which a group of strange characters was gathered.
Zam didn't like the look of them, but the rats
obviously did, because their eyes were all fixed on
the group, their pink rat noses twitching, and their
whiskers quivering with excitement.

There were three very fat cats wearing
wide-brimmed hats. Each had a sword slung from
a shoulder and wore finely made boots with shiny
buckles on their hind paws.

Next to the cats was a group of out-of-towners,

perhaps from the Great Wood,
thought Zam, because their
clothes were all
in different
shades of
green, from
bright lime
to deep, dark
oak leaf. They
wore helmets
with horns
and visors
and feathery
pom-poms, and
were armed to the teeth with
clubs and heavy swords. In the
midst of the group was their
leader, who appeared to be a
girl with golden hair styled
into elaborate curls.

On the other side of
the brazier, which was
piled high with broken
chair legs and splintered
floorboards, stood two
tall tin men. Each one had
glowing eyes that shone in
the gloom of the chamber,
and gleaming metal chests
with glass panels in them,
through which Zam could
see cogs and springs moving,
like the insides of a clock.
Both tin men held enormous
axes in their metallic hands,
and on their shoulders
perched two copper-coloured
beetles with eyes that
glowed as brightly as
their own.

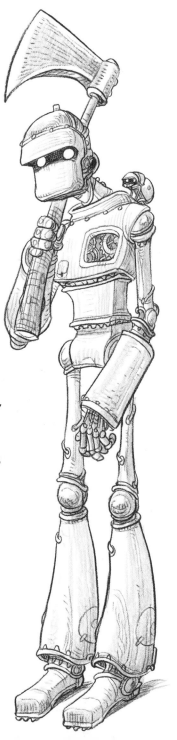

In the very centre of the platform, in front of the brazier, was a large rat with sleek fur and a black velvet waistcoat embroidered with silver thread. Lurking next to him were three others who Zam recognized from the shop: Walters-Walters, Rufus-Rufus and greasy-furred Erics-Erics.

Erics-Erics was clutching the runcible spoon with both hands while the other two held up large matches, ready to strike them on stone and burst them into flame.

'Down with tree magic!' the rats crowding the balconies screeched as Erics-Erics held up the runcible spoon for all to see. 'Burn the spoon!'

The large rat took the runcible spoon and turned it over in his paws before looking at the rest of that strange group. 'Welcome to all who are united against magic!' he began, with a respectful bow to the tin men and the out-of-towners. 'Along with our friends from the Tin Man Timber Company and the Society of Giant-Slayers, not to mention our associates in the Feline Footwear Foundation –' the rat waved a disdainful hand at the fat cats, who bristled slightly – 'the League of Rats has done its utmost to rid our beloved land of Thrynne of dangerous magical objects that threaten life as we know it.'

The large rat raised the runcible spoon, and the others squealed, 'Down with tree magic!' even more loudly.

He went on. 'After all, ever since we ditched the Pied Piper, we've danced to our own tune!

'It gives me,
King Tiberius-
Tiberius,
great pleasure
to commit this
despicable object to
the flames.'

'Burn the spoon!'
the rats chorused as Walters-Walters
and Rufus-Rufus struck the matches and lit the
firewood in the brazier.

Just as the wood started to catch, an enormous
ginger shape launched itself from the top of the
sewer above and landed with a crunch on top of
the tin men. With one blow of his enormous arm,
Ginger swept the squealing fat cats off the platform
and into the pool. With another blow, he did the
same to the giant-slayers and the three rats beside
King Tiberius-Tiberius.

'That's ours,' said a sweet lilting voice, and a

sugar-spun hand grabbed the runcible spoon from the paw of the astonished King Rat while the rats in the balconies squealed in outrage.

Ginger turned, and he and the princess leaped back up into the sewer tunnel above, where Zam was waiting for them.

King Tiberius-Tiberius adjusted his waistcoat as two angry beetles with glowing eyes buzzed above the crushed metal of the tin men, and bedraggled cats and giant-slayers dragged themselves, coughing and spluttering, from the sewer water. The King Rat reached down and grasped Erics-Erics by the greasy scruff of his neck and lifted him up high out of the water and held him dripping at arm's length.

'Tell me again,' he said with icy fury, 'which bakery you stole that wretched spoon from?'

The next morning, Zam was lined up on the parade ground in front of the palace of the Grand Duchess of Troutwine, alongside head baker Balthazar Boabab and the other apprentice bakers. They were ready to start work.

'Bakery No. 9, you're in the calico tent,' the lady-in-waiting to the lady-in-waiting said. 'Washtubs, scrubbing brushes and dish soap are provided, but you'll have to fetch your own washing-up water from the kitchen; we're *far* too busy.'

Not for the first time that morning, Zam looked nervously over his shoulder. He could feel the runcible spoon nestled safely out of sight under his shirt. After the events of the previous day, Zam had spent a lot of time looking over his shoulder.

As soon as they had emerged from the sewers, Zam had smuggled Ginger and the princess back into the bakery, and, not knowing what else to do, he'd hidden them beneath flour sacks in the cellar pantry.

The League of Rats was obviously nervous of the

monster that had attacked them in the sewer, but they were determined to destroy the runcible spoon, and Zam knew it was only a matter of time before they made their move.

All evening, rats had peered in through the windows of the shop, and the scritch-scratch of claws had been heard in the courtyard at the back.

If Bakery No. 9 could just make it through the tea ball, Zam would come up with a plan.

'Washing-up! I hate washing-up,' muttered Langdale, stamping his hoof petulantly, beside Zam.

'Bakery No. 9, to the calico tent!' Balthazar ordered. On the lawns around the parade ground, the other bakeries of Troutwine were setting out trays of delicious cakes and pastries on long tables in front of tents of striped silk with velvet bunting. The apprentices of Bakery No. 12 smirked as Zam and the others trooped past their tables of golden bowls

70

full of deliciously sweet, fluffy floating islands in silky smooth custard.

'Bakery No. 6 is saving all its crumbs for you lot to sweep up!' one of them sneered.

When Zam and the others reached the drab tent next door to the palace kitchens, they found a row of wooden buckets waiting for them.

'At least they've been filled,' said Langdale approvingly. 'Whatever that "high-up" lady said.'

'Everybody, stand by,' said Balthazar. 'When the tea ball starts, there'll be plenty of crockery coming in. Shellac sisters on scrubbing brushes, gnome boys on drying, and you two –' Balthazar nodded to Zam and Langdale – 'on bucket duty. We'll need plenty of refills when we get underway.'

He smiled. 'Come on, Bakery No. 9. I know it's just washing-up, but make me proud!'

Just then, there was a fanfare of trumpets, followed by the sound of twenty harps being delicately plucked. Carriages pulled by beautifully groomed horses began to pull up beside the palace gardens. Soon, from the lawns in the distance came the sound of polite chatter and laughter and the clink of forks on fine china.

'Start collecting plates,' Balthazar ordered Zam and Langdale.

They picked up trays stacked with dirty plates and headed off towards their washing-up station, past the backs of the brightly coloured tents. Zam peered between them and caught a glimpse of the Grand Duchess herself sitting on a high-backed garden chair nibbling some fondant triangles.

'Let's get on with

it,' said Langdale gloomily, as yet another stack of used plates was shoved through the flap at the back of their tent.

Zam picked up the plates, but quickly realized something was wrong. They appeared to be glued together. Just then, there was a shriek, and then another as most of the tea-ball guests on the dance floor slipped and fell over. There was a crash, and Zam glimpsed, through the gap in the tents, several of the tables collapse as their legs snapped in two. Next, he smelt smoke. Flames were licking at the silk tent next to him; smoke was rising from two others.

'Water buckets!' Balthazar Boabab's voice rose above the hubbub. 'Now!'

Zam and Langdale ran back towards the calico tent, only to see Balthazar and the rest of the apprentices of Bakery No. 9 coming the other way, buckets of washing-up water in hand.

As Zam watched, Balthazar and the others surrounded the smouldering tents and threw the water over them. But instead of putting out the fire, they made it much worse.

There was a sudden whooshing sound as the tents burst into flames. In moments, all the tents were ablaze, and the ball-goers were running across the lawns and up into the safety of the palace.

The shocked head bakers of the other Troutwine bakeries turned towards Balthazar and his apprentices as the tent burned amid the wreckage of upturned tables and cake trays. The other apprentice bakers stepped aside as the palace guard in white tunics and tall helmets marched down the palace steps. The Captain of the Guard reached forward and knocked Balthazar Boabab's hat from his head, and two guards seized him by the arms.

'Head baker of Bakery No. 9, you're under arrest on the orders of the Grand Duchess of Troutwine.'

Outside the calico tent, Zam stared open-mouthed. Looking down, he saw one of the remaining water buckets. The water had a glassy, oily film on its surface.

'That's right,' said Erics-Erics, slinking out from behind the tent flap. 'That isn't washing-up water.' He sniggered as he drew out a long, sharp needle and stepped towards Zam. 'Now give me the spoon—!'

Out of nowhere, an expertly aimed hoof knocked the rat off his feet, buying Zam precious seconds.

Langdale's voice sounded in his ear.

'Run, Zam! Run!'

7

THE CELLO

Two weeks later, far away from Troutwine, in the city of Nightingale, Phoebe Limetree knew nothing about Zam and the disastrous tea ball. The young musician opened the shutters and settled on a cushion in the bay of the window. High above, clouds rolled across the sky. Spotting them, Phoebe made a wish: 'To play my own music, just once to an audience,' she whispered. 'Cloud horse, cloud horse, far from view, make this wish of mine come true.'

On fine sunny evenings like this one, Phoebe liked to listen to the sounds of the city. Below her window, there was a rising shimmer as the musicians of the string district began to tune their instruments. Phoebe sat back and closed her eyes, letting the music of Nightingale wash over her.

She had lodged at Fairweather House for a couple

of years now, ever since she'd arrived to train to be a musician. Her landlady, Madame Arpeggio, had been very kind, but on summer evenings like these, Phoebe couldn't help feeling just a little homesick for Spindle Falls. It was a small town, famous for the beautiful soft gruff wool that was spun there. Phoebe's parents raised gruffs on their little farm, and – despite the gruffs' notoriously bad tempers and greedy appetites – Phoebe was very fond of these large, horned creatures. She had often sat in the pasture and played her goat fiddle for the gruffs while they munched on the delicious grass.

Phoebe smiled to herself and opened her eyes. Those days seemed so long ago now, and Madame Arpeggio had taught her so much, here in the hustle and bustle of Nightingale. Below her, rising up through the floorboards, was a screeching sound mingled with the clatter of instrument cases being opened. Phoebe smiled again. It was the cat orchestra: the tabbies, the blacks and the marmalades were getting ready for rehearsals.

Phoebe got up and crossed the room. She reached into the wardrobe and took out a pair of black gruff-wool cat ears attached to a hair band and put them on. Phoebe was an honorary member of the cat orchestra, and she always wore her 'ears' when she played with her friends.

Phoebe glanced over at the window, making sure she wasn't being watched. She listened intently for a moment, then turned back to the wardrobe. She took out a black cello case and opened it.

'Good evening – did you sleep well?' she asked.

'I did,' said the cello. 'But I had the most curious dream . . .'

Phoebe took it out of the case, together with the bow, not at all suprised to find it talking to her.

'What was the dream?' She asked. Phoebe had found the cello at the back of the wardrobe behind a stack of empty shoeboxes only a couple of weeks ago. At first, it had seemed to be just an ordinary cello. When she had mentioned it to Madame Arpeggio, the landlady had been rather vague.

'A cello, dear?' she had said in her tinkling musical voice. Madame Arpeggio was a tiny woman, not much taller than a gnome, and when she wasn't conducting the cat orchestra, she liked to play a little stringed instrument called a slute.

'Yes, I seem to remember we had a spare cello or two around the place, but I really don't know what one is doing in the attic wardrobe,' Madame Arpeggio had added. 'Most odd. But if you take good care of it, my dear, I shall teach you to play it. You won't find it so very different from your goat fiddle. After all, that's why you're here with us, at Fairweather House, to learn to play all kinds of instruments.'

FAIRWEATHER HOUSE

PHOEBE'S ROOM

THE CAT ORCHESTRA'S ROOM

MADAME ARPEGGIO'S ROOM

THE MUSIC STUDIO

THE SALON

THE KITCHEN

COPPER POT ALLEY

It was true. Phoebe's parents had always told her, 'We want so much more than gruff-herding for you. Study hard and make us proud.'

That was all very well, and Phoebe had worked as hard as she could playing her goat fiddle, learning the viola and the double bass before she'd found the cello, but that wasn't the problem. The music the orchestra had to play soon bored her almost to tears. Endless, dreary marches and stomping anthems were all that they were allowed to play, by order of the Clockmaker, who ruled the city.

Only her friends in the cat orchestra and their secret midnight concerts, played very quietly, kept Phoebe from giving up and returning to Spindle Falls. That and another talent she had discovered since arriving at Fairweather House: listening to old pieces of wooden furniture.

She just had to run her fingers lightly over the carved headboard of her little trestle bed to hear it give a soft woody sigh. Her chest of drawers chuckled dustily, and the wardrobe murmured very quietly something Phoebe could never quite catch. Their voices were faint

and wistful, slowly fading beneath the dark varnish along with their memories of the magical Great Wood they came from. But Phoebe loved them.

Then, after just a couple of lessons with Madame Arpeggio, the cello too had begun to speak to Phoebe – shyly at first, and only ever when they were alone. But little by little, they'd become friends.

This was powerful tree magic; Phoebe knew that much. And she knew, also, to keep quiet about it. The townsfolk of Nightingale had learned that tree magic could get you into trouble with the Clockmaker and his tin men, and no one wanted that.

'I dreamed about rats causing mischief in Troutwine . . .' said the cello.

'That was a curious dream,' Phoebe agreed, picking up the bow. She began to comfort the cello by playing a series of soothing chords.

'Thank you,' it said. 'But that's not all. I dreamed of a Piper, an old man with sad eyes and patchwork clothes, who has lost his flute and doesn't know how to find it. He sits alone in a high tower, and his friends no longer visit him . . .'

Phoebe played some more. From the outside, there was a soft whirring sound.

'That's lovely,' said the cello. 'And then I dreamed of a boy with a spoon, running as fast as his legs could carry him. Running, running . . .'

Phoebe stopped playing. She was staring at the windowsill. There was a copper-coloured beetle sitting on the cushion beneath it.

'And then—' the cello began.

'Shh!' whispered Phoebe softly.

8

THE TELL-TALE BEETLE

The copper-coloured beetle scuttled over the cushion and stopped. Its eyes glowed brightly for a moment. Phoebe started playing the cello again, as casually as she could manage, although she could feel her face reddening. The beetle stayed motionless for a moment longer, then twitched as its wing cases flicked open, and its wings whirred. The beetle rose into the air, circled the room, and then flew back out of the open window.

'Do you think it heard us talking?' the cello asked.

'I'm not waiting around to find out,' said Phoebe firmly. She placed the cello back in its case and snapped the lid shut, before leaving the room. She hurried down the stairs to the third floor where she was greeted by the cat orchestra.

A tiny woman holding a conductor's baton was

standing on a chair in front of the cats. She glanced round.

'Ah, Phoebe, my dear, you're just in time for a final run through of "The Timber Wagon March" before the parade later!'

'I'm so sorry, Madame Arpeggio,' Phoebe said. 'I need to

get some pine-pitch for my bow.' She smiled at the cats. 'See you in Clocktower Square, guys,' she called over her shoulder as she continued quickly down the stairs, taking them two at a time.

'Yes, well . . . don't be late, dear! You know what will happen if we are late. We will all be in the most terrible trouble,' Madame Arpeggio's musical voice called after her.

Phoebe rushed past the landlady's rooms on the second floor, the music studio on the first floor, and the salon with its elegant furniture under dust sheets on the ground floor.

Reaching the front door, Phoebe opened it and was only halfway down the steps to the street when she heard the clatter of tin feet on paving stones. Glancing down Copper Pot Alley, Phoebe saw two tin men marching up the hill, axes over their metallic shoulders and eyes glowing. Above their heads, the little copper-coloured beetle hovered, its wings whirring.

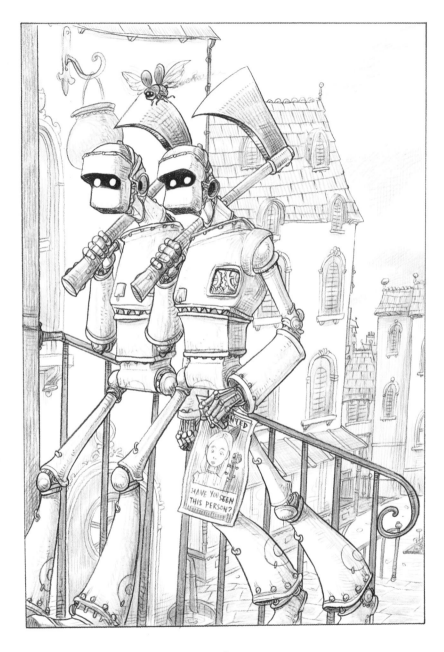

As soon as she reached the bottom of the steps, Phoebe ducked out of sight beneath them. She crouched and watched as two sets of heavy tin boots paused in front of Fairweather House before she heard them thud up the steps to the front door.

Phoebe clutched the instrument case to her chest and could feel her heart beating fast.

The tin men pounded on the door until it opened, and Phoebe heard Madame Arpeggio's voice. 'Can I help you? . . . Oh, I see . . . Well, she isn't here—Wait! Where are you going? This is a respectable musical house!'

The tin men must have pushed the landlady aside, because the next thing Phoebe heard was the sound of their footsteps clumping into the house and up the stairs. The cat orchestra had begun playing 'The Timber Wagon March' but it abruptly halted. The tin men must have reached the third floor. The air filled with howls and hisses as the cats protested at the intrusion, while Madame Arpeggio's voice rose up above the din. 'Everyone, please remain calm! It's just a little misunderstanding. I'm sure you've got the wrong house . . .'

Phoebe felt the instrument case tremble, as if the cello inside was afraid.

'It's all right,' she whispered. 'I won't let them hurt you . . .'

Suddenly the sound of splintering glass made her jump. There was a loud crash, and another. And another. Phoebe peered up from beneath the steps and had to stifle a scream. Lying on its side on the paving stones was her wardrobe from the attic room, and beside it, the chest of drawers and her little trestle bed, legs crushed and headboard cracked. The tin men clattered down the stairs and out into the street.

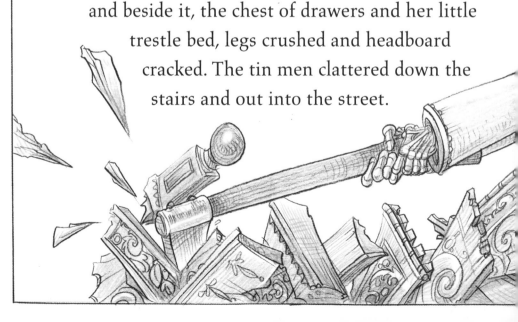

As Phoebe watched in horror, the tin men raised and brought down their axes chopping the furniture into kindling-sized pieces. They gathered the wood into two bundles, tied them with rope, and hoisted the bundles on to their shoulders.

Phoebe couldn't see much more because the scene dissolved into a rippling blur as her eyes filled with tears. She heard the clang of the tin men's boots on the paving stones of Copper Pot Alley, then felt a comforting hand on her shoulder as she sobbed.

'There, there, my dear,' said Madame Arpeggio. 'They've gone.' She helped Phoebe to her feet, and they went back up the steps and into Fairweather House.

The cat orchestra had gathered in the salon, adjusting bowties and smoothing down white jackets, their instruments packed in cases. Madame Arpeggio hurried upstairs while the cats gathered around and gently nuzzled Phoebe, inviting her to stroke the tops of their heads. Generally speaking, the cats of Nightingale were proud and independent, and it was

extremely rare for them to allow humans to stroke them. But Phoebe was part of the cat orchestra, and its members could see that she was upset.

Phoebe dried her eyes on a corner of a dust sheet and stroked Young Possum's head. He was the plump grey tabby who played the other cello. Her poor furniture, smashed up for firewood, Phoebe thought, as she hugged Young Possum, his fur soft against her cheek. Why did the Clockmaker and his tin men hate the ancient trees of the Great Wood? The trees that had magic in them. But she knew why. They didn't like anything they couldn't control, thought Phoebe bitterly. Anything that didn't follow their orders, like clockwork . . .

Now they all had to go to Clocktower Square and play at their awful parade. Phoebe could feel her face flushing with anger. She didn't want to go. None of them wanted to go, but they had no choice. If they didn't follow the rules, the whole orchestra would be in danger, not just Phoebe.

Madame Arpeggio seemed to understand. 'I don't know why the tin men are looking for you, Phoebe – and it's safer all round if we don't know – but you need to slip away unnoticed if you get a chance. For now, the safest thing would be to come with us among the crowds. Here, put this on,' she said gently. She handed Phoebe a black velvet eye mask. 'Now we've got to play in the parade!'

9

THE NIGHTINGALE PARADE

Phoebe walked side by side with Young Possum. Behind her, Sidney and Earnest, the other two tabby cats, carried their double basses in cases slung from their shoulders like shields and kept an eye out for inquisitive beetles.

Up ahead, Madame Arpeggio led the way down Copper Pot Alley and into Woodwind Square. The boys and girls of the Flute School joined them, together with the tall, serious gentlemen of the Long Recorder Academy.

When they reached Trombone Alley, things got a little more chaotic, as the trumblehorn players tried to push the long recorders aside. Madame Arpeggio had to make her way to the front and have a stern word with the band leaders before they could all set off again.

Soon, the procession was making its way up towards the high clocktower that rose above Nightingale's Grand Central Square. As they approached the square, Phoebe saw a tin man pasting a blank sheet of parchment to a wall. As she watched, a copper-coloured beetle with glowing eyes landed on the parchment and scuttled busily across its surface leaving an inky trail.

When it flew off and the tin man marched on, Phoebe gasped. There, on the wall, the ink still wet, was the image of a girl in cat ears holding a cello. Underneath the picture were the words, '*If you see this person, report it to the clocktower, by order of the Clockmaker.*'

Phoebe looked away and pulled the hood of the cape further down over her head. She didn't know what to do. Looking nervously around, heart hammering, she had no choice but to keep going and wait for a chance to escape.

The musicians were marching into Clocktower

Square, and Phoebe could see, from the opposite side of the square, timber wagons arriving to take part in the parade. She also saw pairs of tin men patrolling, beetles flying overhead, their glowing eyes examining the members of bands as they passed. There were more of those posters too, and, not for the first time, Phoebe wondered whether it  would be safer to stay close to the orchestra or try to make a run for it. But how far would she get unless there was some kind of distraction?

The townsfolk of Nightingale were even more closely supervised than the musicians, so it made no sense to mingle with the crowd that lined the square on three sides. Rows of tin men surrounded them. The townsfolk looked glum, but when the tin men,

104

at a signal from a hovering beetle, raised their axes, the crowd cheered and they all waved small flags above their heads. Phoebe decided to stick with the cat orchestra for now.

The procession marched into the square and began to separate into bands in front of the tall clocktower. The tower rose up from the palace that formed the fourth side of the square. The rows of high windows set into the palace walls were all brightly lit, indicating that the Clockmaker was at home and expecting visitors.

High above, the clock struck six. Phoebe, along with everyone else in the square, looked up at its gleaming face. Just below it, a door opened, and a tree cut out of a sheet of gleaming gold metal trundled out, followed by a small figure resembling a tin man with an axe. As the clock struck the hour, the tin man raised and brought down his axe in time to the chimes. On the sixth stroke, the tree folded on concealed hinges and trundled through a door opposite with the tin man following on behind.

Down in the square, the life-size tin men raised their axes, and the townsfolk again cheered glumly. As Phoebe took up her place in the back row of the cat orchestra, she watched the usual timber wagons begin to move into position for the parade celebrating this month's harvest of the trees from the Great Wood. Every month, more and more were felled by order of the Clockmaker. Phoebe sometimes wondered how long it would be before there were no trees left.

At the front of the parade, there were small two-wheelers loaded with logs. Next, came short, stout ponies pulling big flatbeds piled high with freshly cut timber boards from the saw mills of the nearby towns. Behind the flatbeds were the large timber wagons from the Great Wood, pulled by big blue oxen with shaggy coats and huge curved horns strung with lanterns. These large wagons were loaded with the trunks of trees only recently

chopped down, roped together and held down
beneath large sheets of oilcloth. Behind those was a
covered four-wheeler Phoebe hadn't seen before. She
could just make out a painted sign on the side: '*The
Ursine Ballet Troupe of the West*'. It was pulled by
two packhorses with cloth sacks strapped to
their backs.

Finally, the members of the Tin Man Timber Company pushed their way past from behind the wagons and formed into gleaming ranks. There must have been three hundred of them. Taller than the tin men of the town, and twice as powerful, these tin men had bigger axes, saws and hand drills, and four beetles perched on each massive shoulder. It was an impressive show of force.

Just then, a tin man turned from the crowd closest to the cat orchestra and began walking along the row. Phoebe stiffened, and on either side of her, Sidney, Ernest and Young Possum did the same. The tin man's eyes glowed as he looked into each cat's face in turn. Phoebe's grip on her instrument case tightened. The tin man was almost level with her. She looked up into its glowing eyes . . .

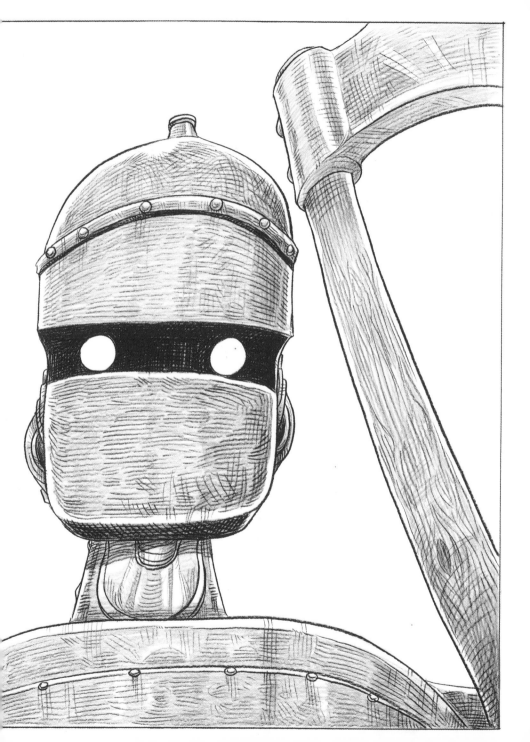

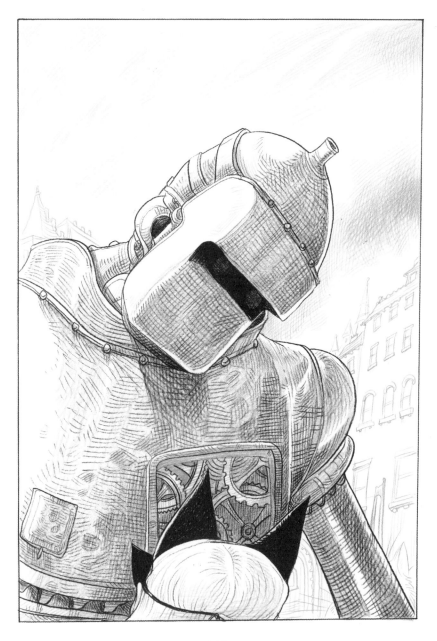

10

PHOEBE LISTENS

As Phoebe looked into the tin man's glowing eyes, they grew dim, flickered and, abruptly, went out. The tin man stood, motionless, its head tilted down towards Phoebe. She looked around – the cats were bristling, and Madame Arpeggio whispered urgently, without turning round, 'Hide, my dear! Quickly, before one of the beetles winds it back up.'

Phoebe didn't need telling twice. The tin man had clearly identified her. She took a couple of steps back, then, head down, she skirted past other groups of musicians before glancing over her shoulder.

A copper-coloured beetle had whirred past Madame Arpeggio and landed on the motionless tin man's shoulder. It scuttled up its neck and disappeared into the small ear-like opening in the side of the head. A clicking sound began as the beetle

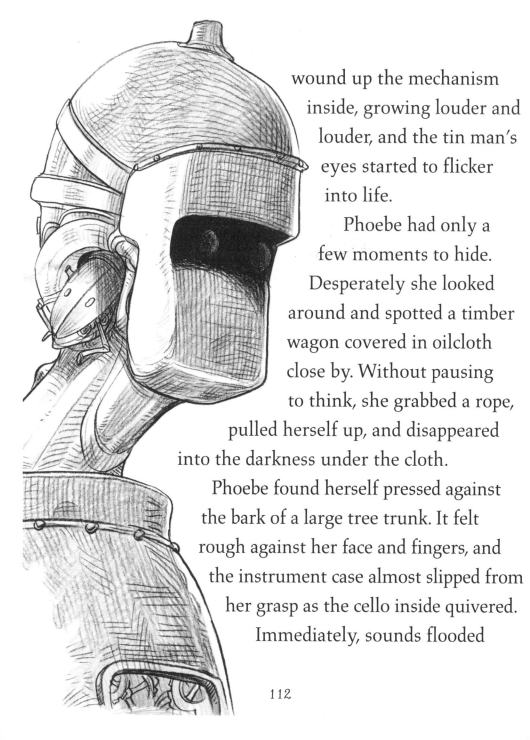

wound up the mechanism inside, growing louder and louder, and the tin man's eyes started to flicker into life.

Phoebe had only a few moments to hide. Desperately she looked around and spotted a timber wagon covered in oilcloth close by. Without pausing to think, she grabbed a rope, pulled herself up, and disappeared into the darkness under the cloth.

Phoebe found herself pressed against the bark of a large tree trunk. It felt rough against her face and fingers, and the instrument case almost slipped from her grasp as the cello inside quivered. Immediately, sounds flooded

Phoebe's head in the darkness: the wind rustling leaves; the creak of branches; the soft whisper of sap rising from roots. Beneath her, the tree trunk seemed to sway and pulse, as if remembering the distant part of the Great Wood it came from. Phoebe lay very still and listened. The tree that this trunk had once been part of was very old. It wasn't the oldest tree in the Great Wood – there were older ones full of tree magic from their roots to the tips of their tallest branches – but it was older than most.

The tree knew many things. Even now, it felt the deep wood around it and far beyond. It felt the footfalls of forest creatures and the footfalls of others. It knew of the great cities and the comings and goings in all of Thrynne like whispers on the wind or the coming of rain. It stood and grew and listened and knew. Thoughts rippled through the tree on into the very heart of the Great Wood where the Forever Tree grew.

Phoebe's head was swimming. Her face rested

against the bark of the tree and felt as though it glowed with its warmth. Outside, the tin men were marching, and the wagons jolted back and forth as the animals pulling them shifted from foot to foot, rattling their harnesses.

Phoebe wasn't aware of any of this. Her head filled with the tree's memories as she pressed her cheek against the bark. The Forever Tree was tall and strong and drew all the magic of the Great Wood up through its roots and into its branches. High in the uppermost branches, where the leaves budded fresh and green, was the nest. And in the nest were eggs . . .

The sound of the bands tuning up brought Phoebe back from the strange dream. She opened her eyes. It was pitch black beneath the oilcloth, and she reached out and pulled a corner aside. The tin man had moved on, and the coast seemed to be clear. She knew she couldn't stay in the wagon. As soon as the oilcloth was removed, she would be caught. She started to form a plan.

The last place the tin men would expect her to be was back with the cat orchestra. So, for now, that was the safest place she could go.

Slowly she eased herself out from under the oilcloth and climbed down from the wagon as the music began.

There was the sound of a whip cracking, and the wagon trundled forward, but not before Phoebe had ducked into the rows of musicians and headed off towards the cat orchestra.

118

11

THE PIED PIPER

'Good to see you again, my dear,' whispered
Madame Arpeggio without taking her eyes off the cat
orchestra, her conductor's baton a blur of movement.
Phoebe slipped in among Young Possum and Sidney
and Earnest, and took the cello out of its case.

The orchestra was in the opening bars of the
Nightingale anthem as an ornate carriage pulled by
eight extremely large white hounds drew up outside
the steps of the palace, and an expensively dressed
woman with a towering hairstyle of blue-grey
stepped out. She must be the Grand Duchess of
Troutwine, Phoebe thought to herself.

The Grand Duchess was helped by a rat wearing
a black waistcoat embroidered in silver. It was clear
by the look on the Grand Duchess's face that she
disliked the rat intensely.

From the back of the carriage, three rats dressed in footman's livery jumped down and attempted to hold the train of the Grand Duchess's dress, only for her to prod them away with the tip of the silver cane she grasped. At the same time, this group was joined by men dressed in different shades of green, wearing helmets and body armour, who were led by a girl with carefully styled ringlets of golden hair.

Phoebe fell into time with the cat orchestra around her, playing the cello part in the rousing Nightingale anthem. As it finished, there appeared to be a minor scuffle as three cats in large boots with shiny buckles arrived in a two-wheeled cart pulled by a bad-tempered gruff, who headbutted one of the footmen rats. The rat, who had rather greasy fur, Phoebe noted, flew over the head of the Grand Duchess and crashed into a cauldron drum with a loud clang.

The cats-in-boots laughed, until the rat in the black-and-silver waistcoat pulled himself up to his full height and stared at them. The cats immediately stopped laughing.

Above the square, a familiar figure emerged on to a balcony. A fanfare blared out and everyone looked up.

The Clockmaker stared down through one of the three pairs of spectacles he was wearing. The other two were pushed up high on his forehead, above a tangle of hair.

'On behalf of the people of Nightingale, I welcome the Grand Duchess of Troutwine, together with the League of Rats, the Feline Footwear Foundation and the Society of Giant-Slayers of Beam to celebrate the latest harvest from the Great Wood.'

He stroked his straggly beard with long, nimble fingers, then motioned for the Grand Duchess to climb the stairs and come up to join him on the balcony. The girl with the golden hair appeared to think that the Clockmaker was motioning to her and rather rudely elbowed past the older woman and ran up the steps.

Pushing and shoving, the men in green, together with the rats and the cats, did the same, leaving the Grand Duchess looking rather lost and bewildered in front of the palace.

Just then, another man climbed slowly out of the carriage and approached the palace steps. He had a full white beard, bushy eyebrows, and white hair so long, it fell almost to his ankles. He wore a battered cap with an ancient white feather stuck in its brim, and faded clothes made up of so many patches, it was impossible to tell what was original and what was a patch. He looked up at the rats disappearing through a door at the top of the steps and his eyes filled with tears. Phoebe felt the cello in her hands tremble.

'That's him!' the cello exclaimed. 'That's the Piper, the man in my dream!'

For a moment, there was silence in the square. Phoebe couldn't tell if anyone else had realized that it was the cello that had spoken. But Madame Arpeggio had. She looked rather shocked, and in a clear attempt at distraction, she raised her baton, and the cat orchestra began 'The Timber Wagon March'. The other bands joined in, and soon

125

Clocktower Square was full of rousing music.

The Grand Duchess climbed the steps with her companion and entered the palace as the timber wagons began to trundle into the square and around the three sides to pass in front of the palace. In front of them, in ranks of ten, marched the tin men of the Tin Man Timber Company. The sound of their boots almost drowned out the music. Meanwhile, on the balcony, the rats, green men and cats-in-boots jostled for the best view, while the Clockmaker stood at the centre flanked by two tin-men attendants, the Grand Duchess and the girl with the golden ringlets.

Phoebe played the cello as loudly as she could. She knew it was sorry for its outburst, but it was no good. Already, three tin men were approaching, with several more behind them. Their eyes were glowing, and they looked fully wound up.

The cat orchestra closed ranks around Phoebe, but they had their backs to a wall, and the tin men were closing in on them. Directly above Phoebe's head, a copper-coloured beetle hovered, giving out a screeching call of alarm.

12

BATTLE OF CLOCKTOWER SQUARE

Suddenly there was a loud roar, and the covered wagon belonging to the Ursine Ballet Troupe of the West swerved past the rest of the parade and screeched to a halt in the middle of Clocktower Square. The flaps covering the wagon flew open, and nine enormous bears in ballet dresses a little too small for them lumbered out, bellowing at the top of their lungs. They charged into the ranks of the Tin Man Timber Company, crushing heads and limbs and sending axes flying.

From the balcony, the Clockmaker pointed to the bears. 'Tin men, stop the lumberers!' he screamed. 'How dare they wreck my parade!'

The tin men surrounding Phoebe and the cat orchestra turned towards the bears, as did every other tin man in Clocktower Square. Raising their

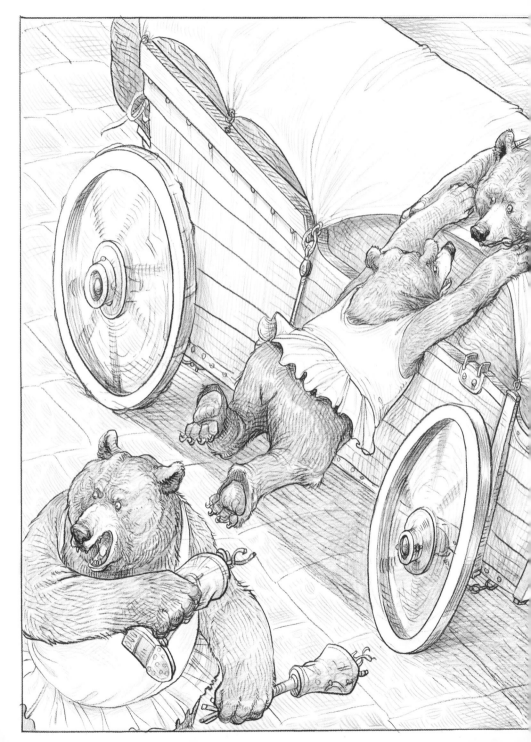

axes, they closed in on the bears, who were causing carnage. At least fifty of the tallest, most powerful tin men already lay in ruins around them. The bears turned on the other tin men, but they were smaller and more agile, and the beetles flying above seemed to be directing them. The bears grabbed broken tin bodies, legs and arms to defend themselves against the swinging axes of the advancing tin men.

Five of the bears ran across to the largest wagon with the tree trunk, the one Phoebe had hidden in, and climbed up on to it, while the other four continued to battle the smaller tin men. They swung their paws, which crushed their metal attackers when their blows landed, but they also suffered from glancing axe blows in the process. The bears on the timber wagon cracked whips, and the blue oxen lumbered into motion. As the wagon trundled past, one more bear broke away and jumped aboard, leaving the last three to keep the advancing tin men at bay.

The largest timber wagon rolled out of the square and headed off through the streets. Phoebe wished she had still been hiding in it. The bears had obviously come to rescue the most ancient of the felled trees from destruction, and, if only she'd stayed, they might have rescued her too.

Back in the square, the three remaining bears were putting up a valiant fight. One had overturned a loaded two-wheeler and was using the logs as missiles to throw at their attackers. The second bear was holding a plank and spinning balletically, sending tin men sprawling in an arc around it. The third grabbed a tin man by the boot and whirled it round and round before letting go and sending the tin man flying through the air, until it shattered on the palace steps. But despite this, there were just too many tin men, and now the bigger, slower tin men were being directed by their beetles to block off the exits from the square.

The three bears started moving back towards their wagon, where the horses were shaking their heads and pawing at the cobbles. Phoebe could see that the bears in ballet dresses were about to leave. They had caused a handy distraction and she would never get a better chance to escape than this. Glancing over at the palace steps, she spotted an empty two-wheeler pulled by a gruff.

It was too far away. Maybe she could get the gruff

to come to her? She softly
began to play one of
the tunes she used to
play to the gruffs
of Spindle Falls.
Immediately it
pricked up its ears,
shook its shaggy
head, and trotted
up to Phoebe,
who tickled it
behind the ears with
the tip of her bow before clambering aboard the
two-wheeled cart. But now what? Her escape route
was blocked.

In the middle of the square, the three remaining
bears had jumped back into their covered wagon,
which was now surrounded by tin men with
glowing eyes.

'Arrest the lumberers!' ordered the Clockmaker.

All of the tin men stepped forward, axes above their heads. Just as it looked impossible for the bears to escape, one of them reached out and pulled the sack bundles from the horses' backs. There was a dazzling flash of white as the sacking fell away to reveal two pairs of magnificent feathered wings. With powerful beats of those wings, the horses took to the air, lifting the bears and the wagon with them.

The whole crowd fell silent at first, stunned by the sight of the beautiful cloud horses.

They flew above the far side of the square, with the wagon dangling beneath them. The bears climbed up the harness traces and held on to the reins before untying the wagon, sending it crashing down on to the tin men blocking the exit from the square below, scattering nuts and bolts, cogwheels and springs in all directions. The two cloud horses flew off towards the evening sun setting over the Great Wood, with the bears hanging on to the reins and waving their paws to the astonished cheering

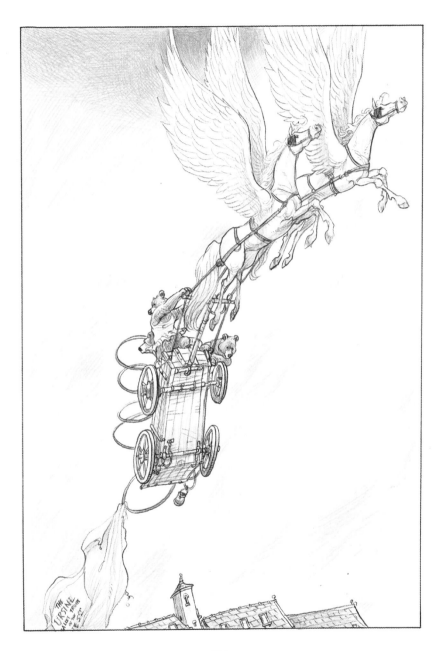

townsfolk. Everyone was looking skywards. No one was looking at Phoebe. This was her chance.

'Goodbye, Madame Arpeggio, and thank you for everything,' she called, as she pulled on the reins. The two-wheeler set off, weaving its way around the piles of crushed tin at the exit from Clocktower Square and off through the streets of Nightingale.

'Goodbye, my dear – and good luck!' Madame Arpeggio called after her.

'Did you see the cloud horses?'

The word is spreading out from Clocktower Square and through the streets and the alleyways of Nightingale and beyond.

'They're real,' they whisper in Troutwine.

'Who would have thought it?' they murmur in Beam.

According to legend, cloud horses hatch in the branches of the Forever Tree, and it is tree magic that gives them wings.

It is said that without the powerful magic of the Forever Tree, cloud horses could not fly.

And without these flying horses, the power of the Forever Tree would be no more.

One cannot survive without the other.

But that was just a legend, a bedtime story . . .

No one believed they were real.

Until now.

BEAM

13

THE GIANT-SLAYER'S DAUGHTER

Meanwhile, far from Nightingale, in the treehouse
town of Beam in the Great Wood, Bathsheba
Greengrass was preparing to leave her home for the
first time. The young orphan closed her notebook
with a sigh. Beside her on the bed, her rucksack was
fully packed and a small kettle and tin cup were
attached to the bottom of the rucksack with string.

The cup had once belonged to her father, Theston
Greengrass, the giant-slayer. Bathsheba couldn't
remember him because she had been only a baby
when he had been stomped on and killed by Olaf
Cloudscraper, the biggest giant ever to venture out of
the wasteland to the east known as the Tumbledowns.

She couldn't remember her mother either, because
she had died not long after her father: some said of
a broken heart; others said from a chill caught after

staying out all night dancing. Whatever the case, Bathsheba was an orphan and had lived ever since in the Boot House Orphanage on the outskirts of the town of Beam in the Great Wood.

The orphanage had been built out of one of Olaf Cloudscraper's boots. The boot was huge – so big, in fact, that it could house Miss Mahalia, the old lady who ran the orphanage, and six orphans, of whom Bathsheba was the eldest. Now it was time for Bathsheba to leave and make her own way in life.

She put on her longcoat and slipped her notebook and pencil into a side pocket. She pulled the rucksack on to her shoulders and crossed to the door of her small bedroom, which was located in the heel of the boot. Above the door was a worpal sword – a traditional weapon used by giant-slayers. Bathsheba had found it propped up against the toe of the boot a couple of weeks earlier, and when it was obvious that no one was going to claim it, Miss Mahalia had let her keep it. It was part of Bathsheba's heritage,

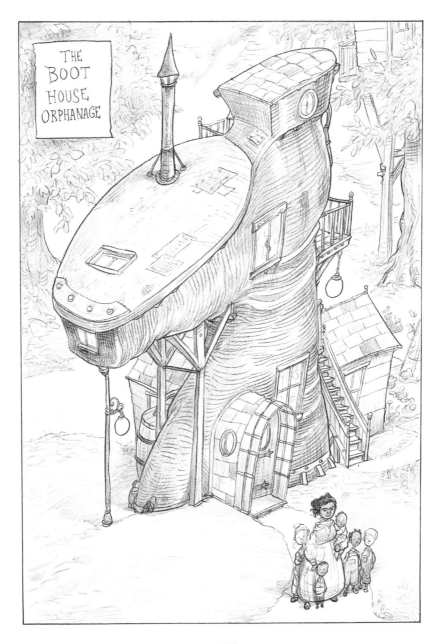

after all, being a giant-slayer's daughter.

She took it down and ran a finger over the leather scabbard and the polished handle of carved wood that sometimes seemed to glow. Next, she attached it to the buckle of her longcoat. Bathsheba took a deep breath, then opened the door and stepped out on to the outside staircase.

Around her, the treetops swayed in the breeze, and the Great Wood stretched out into the distance as far as the eye could see. Clouds drifted overhead and, as she had done since she was little, Bathsheba picked one out and made a wish. 'To find a real living giant,' she whispered. 'Cloud horse, cloud horse, far from view, make this wish of mine come true.'

Now it really was time to go. Fighting back tears, Bathsheba descended the steps, only to find Miss Mahalia waiting for her at the bottom.

'I've baked you some pies, and there are two pots of honey . . .' the old lady began, holding out a neatly tied parcel, 'and a slice of my jub-jub cake – it was always your favourite . . .'

Bathsheba took the parcel and, stooping down, enfolded Miss Mahalia in a great big hug. 'Thank you for everything,' she said, sobbing. 'I'll miss you.'

'Take good care of yourself,' Miss Mahalia said, stepping back to look at Bathsheba, eyes twinkling behind her small spectacles. 'You're a brave, clever girl and I hope you find what you're looking for.'

Bathsheba looked back at the old lady, serious again for a moment. 'I hope so too.'

Bathsheba set off down the main street of Beam. In fact, to call it a main street is overstating matters – it was more of a wide forest path. The town of Beam had been built in the forest; the houses were all tree houses, with walkways and rope bridges connecting them, while below, the paths wound their way around the tree trunks in a series of loops and curves. The only remotely straight path was the main street, which ran from the edge of town to the town square, which was little more than a forest glade with a wishing well at its centre. On market days, the square was packed with stalls and wagons and townsfolk trading their wares; but on other days, it was deserted, except for bored-looking youngsters hanging around the well. As Bathsheba approached

the square, she heard a shout of recognition and her spirits sank.

'Look who it is!' came a voice.

'Well, if it isn't the mouse,' said another.

'Little mousey-mouse is going somewhere, by the look of it,' said a third.

Three girls of about Bathsheba's age stepped out from behind the wishing well, with smirks on their faces. Bathsheba stopped. It was the Beamish girls. All three of them were from respected giant-slayer families, but none as respected as the Greengrasses. The Beamish girls hated Bathsheba for that and spent their time trying to pick a fight. They wanted to become professional princesses like Euphemia Goldencurls, with a crew of giant-slayers working for them, just like she had.

Bathsheba refused to be provoked. They teased her, laughing at her clothes, and called her 'the mouse' because of the way she wore her hair, and because Bathsheba had always ignored them, steering clear of the wishing well whenever possible. But not today. Today, Bathsheba was leaving Beam, and – before she did – she had one last thing to do. This time she was determined to stand up for herself.

The Beamish girls' smirks faded and turned to pouts as they realized that Bathsheba wasn't backing down and hurrying away as she usually did. They unhooked their worpal swords, keeping the blades covered in their scabbards because, as every giant-slayer knows, you only draw your worpal sword to slay a giant. This was just practice. They closed in on Bathsheba, who hoped she appeared braver than she felt. She stood her ground and made herself look

each of the Beamish girls in the eye in turn as her hand closed over the handle of the worpal sword.

It felt surprisingly warm to the touch, and a surge of power flowed up her arm. She unhooked her sheathed sword. Then, quick as lightning, Bathsheba swung it and knocked the first Beamish girl's weapon from her hand. She ducked as the second girl swung at her head and, as she ducked, Bathsheba knocked the girl's legs out from under her with a scything swing of her scabbard. The third girl stood rooted to the spot for a moment, then dropped her sword and ran, followed by her two friends.

Bathsheba couldn't quite believe what had just happened, but she rebuckled her sword and walked out of the square and on through Beam, then into the Great Wood beyond. She didn't look back.

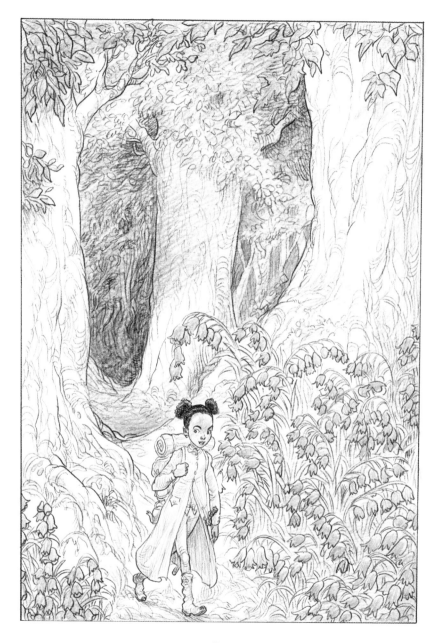

14

THE LUMBERERS

Bathsheba followed the path out of Beam and on into the Great Wood as far as she could. At last, descending a gentle slope into a sunlit dell full of bluebells almost as tall as she was, Bathsheba lost track of the path altogether.

Climbing up the other side, she stood for a moment looking into the dappled depths of the forest ahead. This was what the Beamish folk called the Untrod – the ancient part of the Great Wood where very few humans had set foot before.

All kinds of fantastical forest creatures were said to roam there: giant tree parrots, goat people and their cousins the upside-downers, and lumberers – bears of the ancient wood who didn't bother you unless you bothered them. But what Bathsheba really longed to meet were the giants . . .

GIANT TREE PARROT

She set off into the Untrod, weaving her way under arches of gnarled tree roots and stepping in and out of shards of light that broke through the forest canopy like searchlights. As these turned golden and eventually began to fade, the forest grew darker, until Bathsheba could no longer see the way ahead. She finally stopped in a small clearing and set up camp for the night. She carefully dug a fire pit and was soon using her tinderbox to spark a bundle of kindling with a flint. Blowing softly, Bathsheba teased the smoulder into crackling flame and quickly had a fire going.

GOAT PERSON

She brewed some blue mint tea in her kettle and feasted on Miss Mahalia's 'Monday' pie, followed by jub-jub cake and honey.

Settling down on her unfurled bedroll and using her longcoat as a blanket, Bathsheba opened her notebook and sleepily leafed through its pages.

UPSIDE DOWNERS

LUMBERER

They were full of her own neat handwritten observations taken from *Giants of the Great Wood*, the set of dusty old books chained to the shelves of the Tree House Library. Bathsheba had read them all. For as long as she could remember, she had been going to the library: first, with Miss Mahalia; and later, on her own. It was where Bathsheba had discovered a love of giants and a hatred of giant slaying, which seemed cruel and unnecessary. The yellowing pages of the books, which went back hundreds of years, included records of every giant slain by the giant-slayers of Beam. They also described the appearance, habits and customs of the giants, together with devious ways to trap and slay them.

Bathsheba was less keen on the trapping and slaying. Instead she revelled in the accounts of the giants' activities and enthusiasms. Arguments between the giants had caused

damage to the town that had alarmed the Beamish townsfolk so much, they had clubbed together and sent crews of giant-slayers to settle their disputes once and for all.

That had been the start of the Society of Giant-Slayers, who had set about driving these destructive giants out of the Great Wood. They had been so successful that there were no longer giants anywhere near Beam, and the giant-slayers now had to venture far into the Untrod to slay them. They often had to go even further, as far as the Tumbledowns, where few people ventured. Bathsheba often wondered why, when the giants were no longer a threat to the town.

Bathsheba had a theory that slaying creatures so much bigger than themselves made the giant-slayers feel important and powerful. When they came back from their expeditions, the crews would parade through the town with giant braids of hair, belt buckles and other trophies of their 'heroic' deeds. It made Bathsheba angry.

After reading *Giants of the Great Wood*, Bathsheba believed that the giants didn't mean to be threatening, and she was convinced that if someone had had the courage to talk to them instead of slaying them, then perhaps everything could have been solved without bloodshed.

Unfortunately, that wasn't heroic enough for the Society of Giant-Slayers. Her father, the most famous giant-slayer of them all, wouldn't have approved, but Bathsheba wanted to change things. As the fire crackled reassuringly, Bathsheba's eyelids grew heavy,

and her notebook, full of all she had learned, slipped from her hand. To change things, she thought sleepily, she needed to find giants for herself.

When Bathsheba awoke, her longcoat was damp with early morning dew, and the fire was a pile of grey ash with a few smouldering embers. She was surprised to hear the creak of wagon wheels and the muffled jangle of harnesses. Looking up, she saw a heavily laden, large timber wagon trundling past on the other side of the clearing. It was pulled by two blue oxen, and walking alongside it were at least eight – or possibly nine – large bears in ill-fitting ballet dresses. Lumberers!

Bathsheba pulled her longcoat up under her chin and lay very still with her eyes closed. She knew that if everything she'd read was right, so long as she didn't bother them, the bears almost certainly wouldn't bother her.

Bathsheba couldn't be certain what these
lumberers had been up to, or where they were going,
but one thing was clear: that wagon didn't belong
to them. Bathsheba knew this because, before she'd
closed her eyes, she'd read the lettering on the side
of the wagon: 'The Tin Man Timber Company'.

15

THE PROFESSIONAL PRINCESS

Bathsheba waited until the sound of the creaking timber wagon had disappeared into the distance. As soon as she was satisfied the lumberers had gone, she quickly gathered her belongings and gratefully slipped out of the clearing and into the dappled forest beyond.

She hadn't gone far when she heard music. Someone was playing a beautiful lilting melody on a flute. Bathsheba followed the sound, which seemed to be coming from somewhere up ahead. Eventually, she reached a broad oak tree with rough bark that would provide perfect hand and footholds. Bathsheba climbed up into its branches.

Peering through the leaves, she saw a figure sitting on a fallen tree trunk a little way off. It appeared to be a young woman with fair hair elaborately braided and interwoven with forest flowers. She wore a long flowing blue dress and was holding a small wooden flute to her lips, which she was playing beautifully. Bathsheba stiffened, her hand reaching for the worpal sword buckled to her longcoat. Her fingers closed around the handle while she scanned the forest around the fallen tree trunk. There were large green ferns surrounding it; their umbrella-like fronds concealed the forest floor beneath.

Bathsheba swallowed hard. She recognized the young woman and knew what she was doing. She was Euphemia Goldencurls, the best professional princess in Beam. Bathsheba could feel her face flushing with anger. Suddenly the oak tree shook, and she had to hold on tight to stop herself falling. The tree shook again and again as heavy footsteps approached. The flute music intensified. Ahead of the fallen trunk, a huge hand appeared and parted the branches of the trees to reveal an enormous giant. He stared down at the flute player, his head cocked to one side, a quizzical expression on his lumpy, weathered face.

For a moment, Bathsheba was transfixed, gripping the tree branch and staring, open mouthed. All those hours in the Tree House Library poring over *Giants of the Great Wood,* all those pages of painstaking notes, and this was the first real living, breathing giant she had ever seen.

Euphemia dropped the flute into her pocket and drew a worpal sword from beneath the folds of her blue dress. On that signal, the fern fronds parted, and a harpoon shot up into the air, trailing an uncoiling chain. As Bathsheba watched helplessly, the harpoon struck the giant's hand. Another followed, embedding itself in the giant's shoulder. His eyes widened in alarm, and then his face crumbled into a grimace of pain. He turned, and the forest shook as the giant fled, crashing back the way he had come. The chains attached to the harpoons

went taut, and a wagon shot out from beneath the ferns. Two heavily armed giant-slayers clung on to its sides as the wagon was dragged along in the wake of the wounded giant. As the wagon sped past the tree trunk, Euphemia leaped aboard, brandishing the worpal sword, her red lips parted in a bloodthirsty leer.

Bathsheba leaped down from the branch and hit the forest floor running, her own worpal sword in her hand. She felt a surge of power rising up from the handle and flowing through her body. The giant thundered through the forest, creating an avenue of toppled trees, as the heavy wagon clattered after him.

Bathsheba followed, jumping over tree trunks and flattened ferns. The giant-slayers threw down grappling hooks that snagged on the forest floor and slowed the wagon, making it heavier and heavier to tow. The fleeing giant began to tire and eventually toppled over with exhaustion, his huge chest rising and falling as he battled to catch his breath.

With a cry of triumph, the professional princess jumped down from the wagon, followed by her two sidekicks: a large, stout man with a horned helmet and battered armour; and a small, dapper man with a pom-pom helmet, polished armour and baggy breeches.

'Tam and Shanter,' Euphemia barked, 'take hold of an ear each and hold its head steady . . .'

Bathsheba reached the wagon and slid soundlessly underneath it. She crept forward and cut through the chains that attached the wagon to the harpoons. She looked up. The giant-slayers had got hold of the giant's ears and were twisting them

169

viciously, while the princess stood beside the giant's straining neck and raised her worpal sword.

'I said hold his head steady!' Euphemia snarled.

Miss Mahalia's 'Tuesday' pie – soft, succulent creamed pumpkin in latticed pastry – sailed through the air and hit the professional princess full in the face. She dropped her worpal sword with a surprised squeak and Tam and Shanter let go of the giant's ears in astonishment.

The giant heaved himself up on to his feet and lumbered off into the forest. The princess spluttered as she wiped the remains of the pumpkin custard pie from her face and turned to the wagon. She picked up her worpal sword, and her eyes narrowed to two angry slits as she glared at Bathsheba.

'You!' She spat the word. 'Daddy's little girl.

I might have known it would be you.'

16

THE MAGIC FLUTE

Euphemia Goldencurls hated the Great Wood. It was deep and dark and tangled and so very far from the places she dreamed of: the palaces of Troutwine, the towers of Nightingale . . . She hated Beam most of all – it was so small, the townsfolk so slow-witted and so gullible . . . Although that last one was useful, she had to admit. It had been easy to use the townsfolk's fear of giants to her advantage.

For as long as anyone could remember, the townsfolk had lived in terror of marauding giants flattening their town. Not that this was likely any more. The Society of Giant-Slayers had got rid of most of the troublesome giants years ago – you only had to look in *Giants of the Great Wood* to see that. But giant slaying was lucrative, so the society spread rumours, played on fears, and convinced the townsfolk that they needed the society to protect them. It worked well, and as Euphemia had worked her way up from apprentice to fully fledged professional princess, she had enjoyed admiration and fame.

She had also acquired a rather fine flute from a bedraggled rat she had met in the Giant's Head tavern in Beam. When Euphemia said 'acquired', she meant 'pick-pocketed when the rat fell asleep after too much sweet ale'. The flute's beguiling music had proved irresistible to giants, and Euphemia's career had blossomed.

Unfortunately, to keep her fame and admiration going, the Society of Giant-Slayers had to slay the occasional giant. And even with the flute, this was getting harder and harder to do. It was the part of her job Euphemia hated the most. After all, she wasn't getting any younger, and days and days of sitting in the dismal depths of the Untrod playing the flute in the hope of attracting one of those great

stupid creatures was almost too much to bear.

Another thing that had been too much to bear was not getting the credit. Euphemia had hated that. She had been given her big break in the giant-slaying business by the great Theston Greengrass. His wife had retired to have a baby, so Theston needed a new professional princess to help lure the giants, and Euphemia's flute playing had impressed him. They had slain two giants in their time together – Euphemia had faced the boredom and the danger, and Theston Greengrass had taken all the credit. She could still picture the great giant-slayer parading through the town square with Ogen Bellowbelly's head in his wagon, and beside him, that stuck-up wife of his with little baby Bathsheba in her arms. Euphemia and the rest of the crew had had to follow on behind, listening to the townsfolk's cheers.

So Euphemia had put a stop to that. Some say Theston Greengrass tripped; others that he must have been pushed. But, whatever the case, he had found himself directly beneath a giant's boot when its owner had been stomping through the Great Wood. Euphemia had taken credit for slaying Olaf Cloudscraper and had rewarded Tam and Shanter for staying quiet about Theston's little accident. She had been famous in Beam ever since.

Theston's troublemaker of a wife had suspected something, but a nice fruit basket with a poisoned apple had solved that problem. In fact, Euphemia had even taken the credit for setting up the Boot House Orphanage, although it had actually been that old do-gooder Mahalia's idea to look after little baby Bathsheba, who had been its first orphan.

Bathsheba had grown into a troublemaker just like her mother, so the Beamish girls told Euphemia. Her spies reported that Bathsheba actually said that giant slaying was unnecessary. That sort of talk could ruin Euphemia's plan – and she had big plans. Why else had she visited those smelly sewers in Troutwine and talked to King Rat? She'd even travelled to Nightingale just three days ago to meet the Clockmaker himself.

Now, *he* was a person Euphemia could admire. He and his tin men had no time for the Great Wood and its magic. When he looked at the trees, he saw sawdust for burning or timber for building things – bigger wagons, more magnificent furniture, in even more lavish palaces. With his help, and the King Rat onside, who knows – Euphemia Goldencurls could one day become Grand Duchess of Troutwine . . . Who cares if the Great Wood disappears altogether, so long as she gets what she wants? But there are always troublemakers, and here, standing before her, was just one of these troublemakers: Theston Greengrass's darling daughter, little Bathsheba herself.

Euphemia licked her lips and savoured the sweet taste of pumpkin custard. Bathsheba must have followed their wagon all the way here into the Untrod. Euphemia couldn't help admiring

Bathsheba's nerve, but that wouldn't save her.

She took a step towards the girl, who was holding a worpal sword of her own and staring back at her defiantly. Tam and Shanter had circled round behind Bathsheba: Tam with a heavy mace in his hand, and Shanter with a hammer. Euphemia was furious that the giant had escaped, but it was wounded and wouldn't be too difficult to track.

They were stupid, gullible creatures, as gullible as the Beamish townsfolk, and Euphemia's beautiful flute music would soon lure the giant back to her. Euphemia permitted herself a smile as she raised her worpal sword.

But the smile on her face froze when, seemingly out of nowhere, dark-furred, glittery-eyed bears stepped from dappled shade and surrounded the slaying crew. The lumberers towered over them, low growls rising from between bared teeth. Euphemia and her two giant-slayers looked around wildly. They were outnumbered by too many lumberers to put up a fight. The bears took another step forward, and Euphemia noticed that they were wearing ill-fitting ballet dresses and remembered where she'd seen them before.

'You stole the Tin Man Timber Company's wagon,' she said accusingly. 'In Clocktower Square . . .'

The largest of the bears snarled menacingly, and

Euphemia lowered her sword and backed away towards the wagon. Tam and Shanter did the same, and as the lumberers watched, they took up the traces, embarrassed, and began to push it. The lumberers stepped aside to let them pass, but not before Euphemia had shot a murderous look of hatred at Bathsheba. 'Troublemaker,' she hissed.

17

BUDLEE BRISTLETOE

Bathsheba watched the giant-slayers pushing their wagon through the forest, then turned to thank the lumberers, only to find that they had retreated back into the shadows as silently as they'd appeared.

She sat down on the trunk of a fallen tree and tried to catch her breath. Her heart was thumping, and she felt light-headed after her dash through the forest pursuing the giant-slayers and their quarry. She was pleased that the giant had escaped and wondered who he might be.

Bathsheba took her notebook out and thumbed through its pages. Nobody knew for sure how long giants lived, but all agreed that unless they met a giant-slayer, they lived for a very long time. *Giants of the Great Wood* mentioned giants that had been slain but also giants that had escaped, and some that had just been spotted from a distance. Bathsheba examined her notes, then got out her pencil and underlined an entry.

'*Budlee Bristletoe: grey face, large nose and clear green eyes. Attracted to music, especially the flute. Clumsy and prone to knocking down trees in his path . . .*'

The giant she'd seen fitted this description – perhaps it was the same one?

'*Encountered more than ten times. Not slain.*'

Ten encounters was a lot. Most giants didn't survive so many before the giant-slayers finally trapped them and cut their heads off. Bathsheba couldn't help wondering why Budlee Bristletoe hadn't learned to avoid humans and their music. Some said that giants were stupid and easily tricked, but Bathsheba didn't believe that.

She closed her notebook and got to her feet. Euphemia Goldencurls wouldn't agree with her; Bathsheba knew that much. And, after she had freed Budlee Bristletoe, Euphemia was now her mortal enemy.

Bathsheba patted the worpal sword buckled to her longcoat for reassurance. Going back to Beam wasn't an option now, she realized, even if she wanted to. No. Her future lay in that strange region beyond even the Untrod: the Tumbledowns, where the rich earth of the Great Wood gave way to rocky boulders, which fell away in a tumble of scree that stretched to the east as far as the eye could see. At least, that's how the giant-slayers had described the Tumbledowns in *Giants of the Great Wood*, and Bathsheba had no reason to doubt them. The Tumbledowns was known to be a refuge for misfits. It sounded an extraordinary place, and she wanted to see it for herself.

Bathsheba set off once more. She had one pie left in her rucksack – Miss Mahalia's 'Wednesday' pie, which was a hard-baked pastry envelope containing spiced vegetables and gruff cheese.

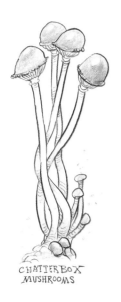

CHATTERBOX
MUSHROOMS

THE
BREADI
BRIGH
SH

That would do for supper, but she needed to fill her water flask at the next forest brook and be on the lookout for edible mushrooms as she walked. Like all the townsfolk of Beam, Bathsheba loved mushroom hunting and was able to identify hundreds of edible varieties that grew around the forest town. There were also others growing in the more ancient parts of the Great Wood that were best avoided, unless you knew enough about them. Miss Mahalia had taught Bathsheba everything she knew, which was a whole lot more than most.

She continued following the trail left by Budlee Bristletoe, if that had, in fact, been the giant's name. After walking for most of the

THE
EAVESDROP PUFFBALL

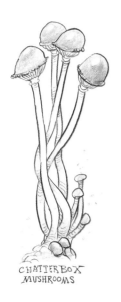

THE UNTHINKING CAP

day, she came across the harpoons, snapped in two, with their points stuck in the ground near some mossy rocks. Judging by the traces of blood and bare patches on the rocks, Bathsheba could tell that the giant had managed to pull out the harpoons and dress his wounds. After this, the trail of snapped branches and toppled trees ended, suggesting that the giant was in less pain, which made Bathsheba hopeful that he wasn't too badly injured.

That night, as she made camp and settled down on a soft bed of moss, too tired to make a fire or even eat more than a few mouthfuls of 'Wednesday' pie, Bathsheba patted her rucksack contentedly. It was full of the mushrooms she had gathered on her journey. In the morning, they would make a delicious breakfast, Bathsheba thought, as she drifted off to sleep.

18

A TUMBLEDOWNER

Bathsheba had the strangest dream. She was
on a timber wagon, surrounded by lumberers.
The wagon swayed and jolted as it made its way
through the forest. Bathsheba looked into the
glittery eyes of the dark-furred bears sitting
beside her in the wagon. They snarled at her, their
white fangs flashing. Only, Bathsheba suddenly
understood, the lumberers weren't snarling; they
were smiling at her.

'Where are we going?' she asked calmly, safe in
the notion that this was just a dream. The wagon
gently swayed as it trundled on.

'We're going deep into the heart of the Great
Wood, little one,' said the large lumberer holding the
reins of the oxen. 'It is the most ancient of all the
ancient parts of the forest.'

'And why have you got this?' Bathsheba stroked the bark of the tree trunk she was sitting on. The wagon swayed back and forth. 'Euphemia said you stole this from the Tin Man Timber Company.'

'You can't steal something that belongs to you,' the bear growled, and Bathsheba could tell it wasn't smiling. 'This is ancient timber, full of tree magic,' the lumberer continued. 'It belongs to the Great Wood. It was cut down by the mechanical axes of the tin men. We have reclaimed it. The tin men won't stop their chopping, no matter how many trunks we lumberers reclaim. They get closer to the Forever Tree every year, eating into the heart of the Great Wood. There are too few of us to halt the army of tin men timberers.'

'What are you going to do with it?' asked Bathsheba, clinging to the tree trunk as the wagon shook and juddered.

'The ancient wood has powerful magic. It can be worked and turned into useful things. See for yourself,' said the lumberer, pointing a claw.

Bathsheba looked down. Buckled to her longcoat was her worpal sword, the handle glowing brighter and brighter with what she now realized must be tree magic. At that very moment, the wagon gave a violent lurch sending Bathsheba tumbling backwards and . . .

She opened her eyes and sat up with a start. In front of her was a great jumble of rocks and boulders, stretching off into the distance as far as the eye could see. For a moment, Bathsheba thought she must still be dreaming, but then her tummy rumbled, and she felt a cool breeze on her face. Her worpal sword and the rucksack full of mushrooms were next to her. The handle was no longer glowing. Bathsheba stroked the soft moss she was sitting on – only now, in the daylight, it looked less like moss and more like . . .

'Hair!' Bathsheba exclaimed.

The ground beneath her swayed – except it wasn't

ground at all. Bathsheba leaned forward and found herself looking down over a forehead and two bushy eyebrows into a pair of enormous eyes.

'Good morning. I'm Bathsheba Greengrass,' she said, trying to control the tremble in her voice and act calmly as if it were the most natural thing in the world to wake up on a giant's head. 'What's your name?'

'My name,' said a surprisingly soft, gentle-sounding voice, 'is Grizell Barkfire, and I'm as old as the hills. Please, please don't slay me.'

'I wouldn't do that!' protested Bathsheba. 'I love giants. In fact, I've been waiting to meet a giant for as long as I can remember . . .'

'So that you could slay it?' asked Grizell, and Bathsheba felt a tremble run through the giantess's body.

'Certainly not!' she said.

'But you have a worpal sword,' pointed out Grizell, frowning up at Bathsheba.

'That's true,' admitted Bathsheba. 'But I would never use it that way. I think giant slaying is wrong.'

'You do?' said Grizell, looking puzzled for a moment. 'I thought it was strange after you captured me that you just went off to sleep.'

'I didn't capture you.' Bathsheba couldn't help chuckling. 'I mistook your head for a boulder and your hair for soft moss last night in the dark. I was very tired. Would you mind putting me down on the ground? Being up this high is making me very dizzy.'

'That explains a lot,' Grizell muttered, holding a hand to her forehead and allowing Bathsheba to step on to it. The giantess placed Bathsheba carefully on the ground. 'I suppose it's my own fault, really. I just lay down for a few moments to rest when you trod on my hair and started picking mushrooms. Then you climbed on my head and fell asleep. I thought if I could just tiptoe as far as the falls without waking you, I could wash you out of my hair and escape.'

'I'm so sorry I frightened you,' said Bathsheba. 'I hope we can be friends.'

'I'm not sure about that,' said Grizell, stepping back and taking a long hard look at Bathsheba. 'After all, this could be a trick, and any moment now, your giant-slayer crew could come sneaking up behind me . . .' Grizell's eyes widened in panic as she looked over her shoulder at the fringes of the forest behind her.

'I don't have a crew,' Bathsheba said, sitting down on a boulder that was definitely a boulder, and taking out her notebook. 'In fact, yesterday, a gang of lumberers rescued me from a crew of giant-slayers . . .'

'You're a friend of the lumberers?' said Grizell, impressed.

'I hadn't thought of it like that, but yes, I suppose I am,' Bathsheba said with a reassuring smile. She looked around her. 'We seem to have come a long way while I was asleep. Where are we?'

They were on the edge of the Great Wood, where the rich earth of the forest gave way to stone, and boulders tumbled down in great towering piles of scree. To the north lay the great city of Troutwine, while to the south, beyond the Great Wood, was Nightingale. To the west was the small forest town of Beam with its fearful townsfolk and blustering giant-slayers. Bathsheba wasn't going to miss her old home.

She had never quite felt she'd fitted in there. She'd always seemed like a misfit in Beam because of her attitude to slaying. It was very hard to make friends when you were so different from everyone else and, sometimes, she'd felt very lonely. Now she'd already made friends with the lumberers and Grizell. Things were changing for Bathsheba.

She patted the boulder next to her, looking encouragingly at Grizell. 'Now why don't you sit down here and tell me about yourself?'

GIANTS of the GREAT WOOD

GRIZELL BARKFIRE

BUDLEE BRISTLETOE

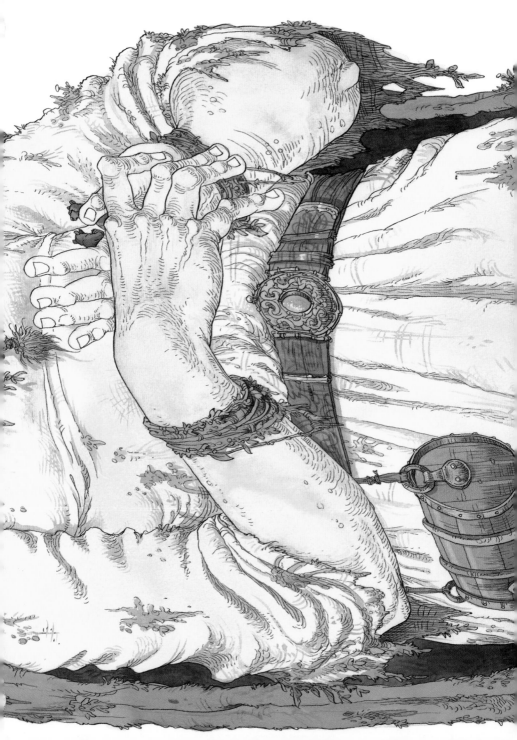

OLAF CLOUDSCRAPER

FINBLAD CRIMSTONE

EBNAH
TREEBROWS

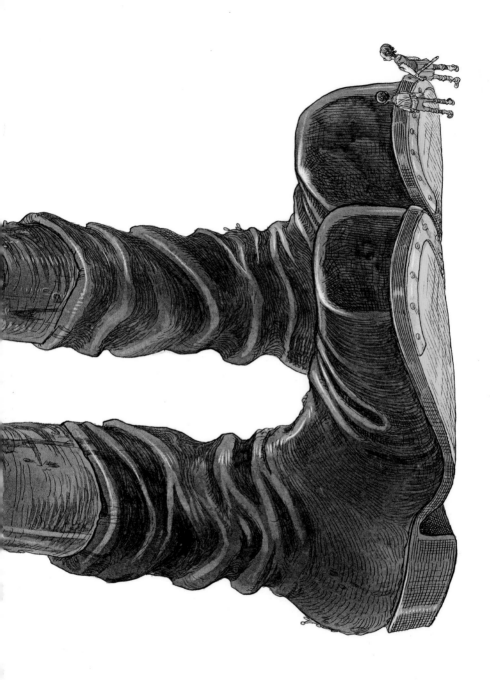

FRENELLA
AND
BROTHE
SLUGHORN

MOTE
MULCHFOOT

Grizell Barkfire sat down, arranging her robe of woven wood strips covered in sprouting ferns and forest flowers. Her moist green hair fell in cascades from her shoulders to her coracle-sandalled feet. Bathsheba smiled.

She was exactly where she wanted to be: no longer a Beamish girl, but instead a Tumbledowner.

19

BOCKLIN'S STORY

Deep in the Tumbledowns Zam Zephyr sat back in his chair and admired the well-stocked shelves here in the underground cavern kitchen. He polished the runcible spoon thoughtfully with the corner of his apron and put it back in his top pocket. The spoon had really changed Zam's life, he didn't mind admitting it. He closed his eyes and allowed his thoughts to drift back to that fateful day, just a few weeks ago, when the League of Rats had sabotaged the Grand Duchess of Troutwine's Tea Ball, and everyone had blamed Bakery No. 9. Again.

As the palace guards in their white tunics and tall, plumed helmets had marched down the steps into the gardens and arrested Balthazar Boabab, the rats had scuttled back into the sewers. Zam had run down the steep, sloping streets from the palace and into the winding alleys of the Lower East Side.

Reaching Bakery No. 9, Zam let himself in by the back door and crept down into the pantry. The bakery was quiet – there were no sounds of rats' claws on the floorboards above – but Zam knew he didn't have much time. He picked up two flour sacks and entered the flavour library.

'Need some help?' said a soft voice, and looking down, Zam saw the sugar-spun princess looking back up at him. Behind her loomed Ginger.

'Here,' said Zam, handing them the flour sacks. 'Fill these with as many jars as you can.'

He grabbed another flour sack and went over to the chest of drawers and began filling the sack with recipe parchments and any useful equipment or ingredients he could find. When the sacks were full, the sugar-spun princess helped Zam tie them up and secure them to a broom handle. Ginger lifted the broom to his shoulders as effortlessly as if the bulging sacks were filled with feathers, then scooped up the sugar-spun princess. They stood for a moment, looking down at Zam.

'Now what?' asked the princess.

'We get out of the city,' said Zam. He hoped he sounded decisive, but the truth was he wasn't sure where to go. His world was crumbling around him like an over-dunked biscuit in tear-water tea. Zam needed order and a clear plan to feel confident, but things were just moving too fast.

'I've saved as much as I can, and I'll keep it safe while we work out how to rescue Balthazar,' he added.

Ginger gave a deep, gurgling groan.

'According to Ginger, the spoon says we should head for the Great Wood,' said the sugar-spun princess.

'Well that's as good a place as any,' said Zam, patting his top pocket, and feeling a little better.

They left the bakery by the back door and stepped out into the alley.

'Well, well, well!' came a sneering voice.

Zam spun around. Blocking the alley were at least twenty rats, with Erics-Erics at their head. He smoothed down his greasy fur and raised a catapult. 'We've come for the spoon,' he said.

Zam turned to run, only to find the way blocked by twenty more rats, led by Rufus-Rufus, his catapult at the ready.

'And this time, your gingerbread friend can't save you,' added Walters-Walters.

The rats trained their catapults on Ginger. Zam noticed that they were loaded with glistening pink balloons. 'Water bombs,' said Rufus-Rufus, chuckling. 'Guaranteed to turn your friend here into soggy biscuit crumbs.'

Zam reluctantly reached for his top pocket. Inside it, he thought he could feel the spoon tremble.

'Don't do it,' pleaded the sugar-spun princess. 'You run – we'll go down fighting.'

Just then, there was a loud clang, and the grille covering the sewer in the back alley flew open.

Out came a water badger in a leather coat and cap, swinging a large oar. Rats went flying, and their water bombs burst as they dropped their catapults. Ginger did a galumphing dance, avoiding the puddles.

'Down into the sewer. Quickly!' said the badger, batting away flying water bombs. Zam and Ginger, with the sugar-spun princess on his shoulder, climbed down into the sewer, followed by the badger who clanged the grille shut behind them. He threaded a padlock between the bars and snapped it closed. 'That should hold them for a while,' he growled.

'We'll hunt you down!' shouted Walters-Walters from the alley. 'Nobody escapes the League of Rats!'

Waiting below was the water badger's barge. Zam recognized it from his last visit to the sewers.

'Bocklin is the name,' said the water badger, helping Zam aboard. 'I'm the sluice keeper. Seems you've got on the wrong side of our ratty friends – never a good thing in this city of ours, believe me.'

Ginger stepped reluctantly on to the barge, eyeing

the water warily. He was coaxed on board by the sugar-spun princess whispering in his ear.

'How did you know we needed help?' asked Zam. He settled himself down on a clump of reeds only for the river sprites to start flapping around him, the leafy tendrils on their hats quivering.

'Mind the reedlings!' cautioned Bocklin. 'They need planting upriver to keep the waters clear.

'As for that runcible spoon of yours, word travels fast in the sewers. It has powerful tree magic in it, probably carved from Forever wood.'

The badger continued powering the barge forward with strokes of the oar, which seemed to glow softly in his paws. Looking down, Zam saw that the runcible spoon was glowing too. Bocklin smiled at him.

'My oar is crafted from ancient wood, though not as powerful as your spoon. It has served me well since the League of Rats took over. I do my best to clean up the mess they make and keep the sluice gates clear. I usually stay out of the rats' business,

207

but they're getting worse, and when I heard the commotion up above, I had to help.

'Rufus-Rufus and Erics-Erics are bullies,' he continued. 'But the rats aren't all bad, you know. Once upon a time, before the waistcoats and the cakes, the rats were forest creatures, loyal and kind and full of stories . . .' Bocklin frowned. 'But they changed when they lost their leader . . .'

'But I thought the King Rat, Tiberius-Tiberius, was their leader,' said Zam.

'He is now, but it wasn't always that way. We've got a long journey ahead of us. I'll tell you the story on the way. Make yourself comfortable,' said Bocklin, guiding the barge through the dark sewers. 'I can take you as far as the North River Falls,' he said. 'To the Tumbledowns. Then you're on your own.'

The water badger had been as good as his word, and soon, they had passed through the sewers and out into the river beyond. By the time they'd arrived at the North River Falls, Bocklin had told Zam all about the Pied Piper, who'd been the rats' greatest friend. He'd charmed them with his flute music, and they'd loved him. But then they'd come to Nightingale, the Piper had fallen in love with the Grand Duchess and he'd lost his flute. It had all gone downhill from then.

Bocklin guided his barge to the riverbank and helped them ashore. Ginger had been grateful to climb off the barge and away from the water. The sacks on the end of the broom handle had swayed as he'd clambered over the tumble of boulders.

Zam had stood on the riverbank and waved to the barge as it glided away, calling his thanks to the badger and the sprites. Then, turning away, he had caught up with Ginger and the sugar-spun princess who were standing on one of the boulders. It was only then that Zam had seen they weren't alone.

Standing a little way off was a giantess with long, flowing green hair festooned with mushrooms.

20

PHOEBE'S MUSIC

Phoebe Limetree sat down on the boulder and looked out across the Tumbledowns. They were incredible. It was like sitting on the shore of a sea of stones.

It had been a long journey from Nightingale. As Phoebe had fled from Clocktower Square clutching her cello, she had heard the metallic clatter of the tin men behind her. She hadn't looked back. Instead, the gruff and cart had sped her through the maze of back alleys and winding streets until they'd found the road out of the city to Spindle Falls.

Phoebe longed for home and for freedom, to be somewhere she didn't constantly have to look over her shoulder because she was being watched.

She had travelled through the night, the full moon above her like a silver lantern, until she had seen the safety of the blue thatched rooftops of her home town ahead. But Spindle Falls had changed. As she skirted the edge of town, Phoebe had been alarmed to see tin men everywhere, gleaming axes on their shoulders as they clanked down the streets. Next she had seen the posters. They were everywhere too – pasted on walls, doors and window shutters. There she was, looking back at herself from the posters, her likeness captured by those copper-coloured beetles. With a sinking heart, Phoebe had realized that she couldn't go home. Rather than making her parents proud, she risked getting them thrown into prison alongside her if the tin men found her hiding in their cottage. She had no choice but to keep running, and the only way she could now was into the Great Wood.

As the sun rose over the falls, Phoebe had known she didn't have much time. She couldn't take the gruff any further so she'd tied it up beside the well. She then borrowed a basket and filled it with anything she could find: cooling loaves from the back door of the bakery; carrots and sweet turnips

from her mother's allotment; a clutch of eggs from the chicken coop and a warm blanket from the clothes line.

Tying the basket to her back, Phoebe had set off into the Great Wood, heading north. Perhaps Troutwine was somewhere she could find work and escape the tin men? She had to try.

That had been three days ago, and now Phoebe's supplies had run out. She had enjoyed walking from glade to glade, climbing the tallest tree she could find each night and sleeping in its branches. She wasn't afraid, as she'd thought she might be, all alone in the forest. The trees seemed like guardians, and Phoebe felt safe among them. She listened to their gentle whispers when she reached out to touch their bark. And when she slept, Phoebe had dreamed of bears and winged horses and flying high through the clouds, looking down at the Great Wood below.

At last, her stomach rumbling, Phoebe had emerged from the forest to find the lonely desolation of the Tumbledowns spread out before her. If she was ever to get to Troutwine, Phoebe knew she'd have to climb down over this sea of stones. First, she needed some music to lift her spirits for the journey.

The cello had remained quiet in its case as Phoebe had walked, but now she clicked open the catches of the instrument case and took it out.

'Hello,' it said. 'I've had the most wonderful dreams.'

'So have I,' said Phoebe. 'I'll tell you about mine if you tell me about yours. But first, let's play.'

'What a good idea,' said the cello. So Phoebe played. For the first time, in a long time, she wasn't being forced to play a particular tune or piece of music; she just played what seemed to be inside her wanting to come out. The freedom was wonderful. She played the murmurs of the trees, the dabbled sunlight of the glades, and, most of all, she played her dreams of dark-furred bears and magnificent cloud horses. The music swelled over the Tumbledowns and into the far distance . . .

Suddenly a shadow fell across the boulder Phoebe was sitting on. She looked up and froze. Staring down at her was an enormous giant with long, flowing green hair the colour of moss, dotted with sprouting mushrooms. The giant's face creased into wrinkles as it bared its fangs.

Phoebe screamed, then leaped up and fled across the jumble of boulders in panic, trying not to bash the cello as she ran. She jumped from one rock to the next, sending others tumbling down over the scree as she did so. Phoebe glanced back over her shoulder. The giant wasn't chasing her; instead it was standing still, open mouthed, a look of astonishment and disappointment on its craggy features.

Phoebe turned back and leaped towards the next boulder, only to see a girl step out from behind it. The girl was holding a glowing sword, which she raised above her head menacingly as Phoebe landed.

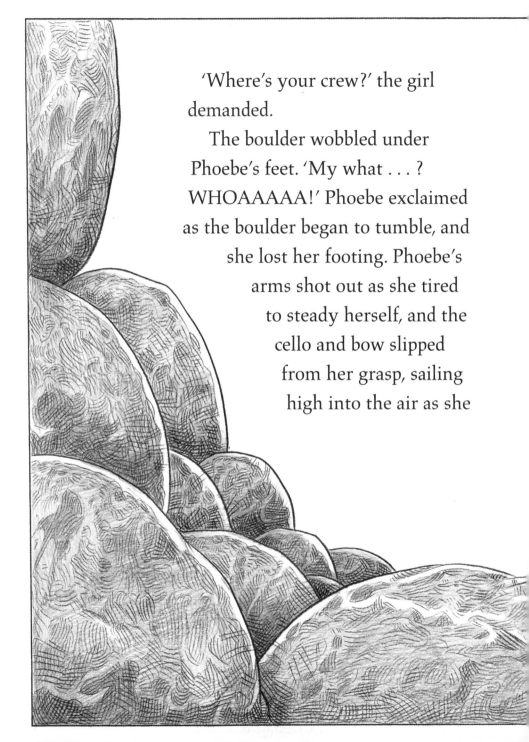

'Where's your crew?' the girl demanded.

The boulder wobbled under Phoebe's feet. 'My what . . . ? WHOAAAAA!' Phoebe exclaimed as the boulder began to tumble, and she lost her footing. Phoebe's arms shot out as she tired to steady herself, and the cello and bow slipped from her grasp, sailing high into the air as she

fell down into the ravine that had been revealed
by the tumbling boulder. Phoebe caught a glimpse
of the girl catching the cello and the bow before
the darkness swallowed her whole.

21

GINGERBREAD PEOPLE

Phoebe opened her eyes. She felt dizzy, and when she reached up to touch her forehead, she winced with pain. Her hair was sticky with what she assumed must be blood; it was too dark to be sure.

She sat up with a low groan. She had lost her cello. That girl with the glowing sword had it now. Phoebe had to get out of here, wherever *here* was, and rescue the cello. Tree magic was feared and misunderstood – Phoebe's experiences in Nightingale had taught her that – and if the cello started speaking, who knew what trouble would follow? And yet, Phoebe couldn't help wondering about that girl's sword . . . She had only glimpsed it, but there was something about it that she recognized. She just wasn't sure what. Phoebe decided to think about it later when her head wasn't aching so much.

Just then, a glow lit up the walls around her, and Phoebe saw that she was in a cavern of some sort. The glow grew brighter, and Phoebe saw a strange procession approaching, holding lanterns. As they drew near, Phoebe saw that they were small gingerbread figures of the sort she'd seen on bakers' stalls in Nightingale. But unlike those sweet, flat cookie-cutter biscuits, these gingerbread figures were rounded and dumpy, with small spoons and forks for fingers, and faces that had carefully modelled features baked into them. But more extraordinary than any of that, these gingerbread figures appeared to be alive. They surrounded Phoebe, raising their lanterns above their heads as she got awkwardly to her feet.

One of the gingerbread figures stepped forward. He was a boy with large icing-sugar eyes and spun-sugar hair. He raised a hand with three teaspoon fingers to Phoebe.

'You want me to go with you?' she asked.

The gingerbread boy nodded and clinked his teaspoon fingers together. Phoebe took his hand and followed as the gingerbread people formed a single file ahead of her, and marched through a small arched opening on the far side of the cavern. Phoebe glanced up and saw that the cavern wasn't solid but was formed from the boulders of the Tumbledowns wedged together. She had fallen through the spaces between.

She ducked her head as she walked through the opening and down a winding stone tunnel that must have been chiselled through the middle of a gigantic boulder. At the other end of the tunnel, Phoebe stepped out into another cavern, lighter than the first, and far bigger. Looking up, she could

see the sky through the narrow spaces between the boulders.

The line of gingerbread people filed down another tunnel, and Phoebe followed, clutching the gingerbread boy's hand for support. She was still feeling dizzy, and, unlike the gingerbread people – who were all different shapes and sizes, though none as tall as her – she had to bend low to avoid hitting her head again. Some were tall and thin, baked dark; others were round and plump, light ginger or speckled. But there was one thing the gingerbread people did have in common – a delicious biscuity small, warm and spiced. It made Phoebe feel safe and cosy and very, very hungry.

They passed through several more caverns, and Phoebe noticed nests lodged in crevices, several wooden cabins built on ledges high up in the gaps between the boulders, and once, hammocks strung across similar gaps, with pots and pans and bedrolls hanging from them. She wondered who else besides the gingerbread people had made the Tumbledowns their home.

Phoebe was just pondering this when the gingerbread people came to a halt. The tunnel they had entered was blocked by a large boulder. The gingerbread boy tugged on Phoebe's hand and pushed his way to the front of the line. Reaching out, he knocked on the boulder with his teaspoon fingers. There was a scraping sound, and the boulder slowly rolled aside. Phoebe felt a blast of hot air as she stepped through the opening and looked about her.

She was standing in a cavern kitchen lined with stone shelves crowded with cooking utensils, sacks of flour and sugar, ingredients in jars, pots and bottles, and firewood stacked in neat bundles. In one corner was a large stove with a stone chimney and a hob cluttered with simmering pots and pans. Below the hob were eight oven doors, their round windows glowing brightly.

The kitchen was bustling with white-aproned

figures stirring cake mixture, kneading dough and washing bowls.

The gingerbread people flooded past Phoebe and, blowing out their lanterns and stacking them neatly by the door, grabbed tiny brooms and dustpans and began sweeping the floor.

'So pleased you could join us, at last,' said a soft, lilting voice, and Phoebe looked down to see a small figure standing at her feet. 'I'm the sugar-spun princess, and this is Ginger.'

Standing behind the princess was a huge gingerbread figure. 'We know someone who will be eager to meet you,' she continued with a smile. 'Please follow me.'

Phoebe smiled weakly. The kitchen was warm, and all the activity was making her head swim. It was beginning to feel like one of her dreams from the Great Wood. She followed the sugar-spun princess and Ginger up a staircase that wound its way round the walls of the cavern until they reached a small balcony. Phoebe saw a door in front of her with a sign on it that read *'The Flavour Library – Please Knock and Come In'*. So Phoebe did as it said.

22

THE FLAVOUR LIBRARY

Phoebe sat down gratefully in the chair Zam offered her.

'I'm Zam Zephyr from Troutwine,' he said. 'That's a nasty bruise you have there.'

'Phoebe Limetree,' said Phoebe weakly. 'From Nightingale . . . A giant scared me, and I fell . . .'

Zam smiled as he crossed the room and began looking through the jars on the shelves. He selected a few and poured their contents into a small bowl. Phoebe couldn't help noticing how tidy and well ordered everything looked.

'Giants are more scared of you than you are of them,' he said. 'And I should know because giants were the first people I met here in the Tumbledowns.'

Phoebe touched her forehead and winced. 'The Tumbledowns . . . Yes, I remember now. There was a girl holding a sword, and its handle was glowing . . .'

'Glowing?' asked Zam, looking thoughtful and pouring the contents of the bowl on to a towel, which he folded and pressed against Phoebe's head.

'I dropped my cello, and she caught it as I fell.'

'Cello?' said Zam.

The towel felt deliciously cool against Phoebe's head, and the pain seemed to melt away.

'Are you going to just repeat everything I say?' she asked.

'What sort of wood was the sword handle made from?' asked Zam, ignoring her question. 'Did it look the same as this?' He took the runcible spoon from his top pocket.

Phoebe sat up in her chair and the towel fell into her lap. Now that her head no longer hurt, her thoughts were clear. 'You,' she said softly. 'You're the boy with the spoon. You ran away – my cello had a dream about you.'

'Your *cello* had a dream?' Zam looked surprised.

Phoebe nodded. 'It's a magical cello. It talks to me. That's how we got into trouble in Nightingale. Tree magic isn't allowed there by order of the Clockmaker, so I had to get away. It was too dangerous to stay.'

Zam sat down opposite Phoebe and thoughtfully turned the runcible spoon over in his hand.

'I found this spoon in my bakery in Troutwine. I didn't understand at first, but it has tree magic too. Anything I stir and make with it comes to life . . .'

'So you baked those gingerbread people?' said Phoebe, wide-eyed. 'And the little sugar girl?'

'The sugar-spun princess,' said Zam. 'That's right. I made her and Ginger first, before I understood what the spoon could do. We had to run too. The League of Rats wanted to burn the spoon and we had to escape from Troutwine.'

'I saw rats in Nightingale!' said Phoebe excitedly. 'They were with the Clockmaker and his tin men.'

'Tell me everything,' said Zam.

So Phoebe did. And, in turn, Zam told her about

the rats, the Grand Duchess's Tea Ball, escaping from Troutwine and arriving in the Tumbledowns.

'That's when I met Grizell Barkfire,' Zam

continued. 'She introduced me to other giants, and they gave me their kitchen cavern to use. It needed a lot of tidying, but I enjoy that. I had a lot of help too, not just from the giants. You saw some of the others down in the kitchen.' Phoebe nodded.

THEODORA

'Wensley and Airdale are goat boys from the Western Mountains; Theodora is a river sprite from a pool below the North River Falls; and I'm not sure where Arnie and Kat are from originally. They may be an owl and a cat, but they're my best bread bakers. You see, the Tumbledowns seem to collect those of us who've run away from places where we don't quite fit in.'

Phoebe nodded again.

'Bocklin the water badger brings us all the flour, eggs and sugar we need from Troutwine,

WENSLEY   AIRDALE

ARNIE   KAT

and the giants bring firewood and forest fruits from the Great Wood, and, in return, we bake them daily bread. Bocklin has also just taken our first batch of pastries and cakes to Troutwine, where they have been very popular, although no one knows where they're from,' Zam added with a smile.

'What about the runcible spoon? Where do you think it came from?' asked Phoebe.

Zam frowned and looked down at the spoon in his hand. 'I'm not sure,' he said slowly. 'It's a mystery. I know it has tree magic, but I don't know how it came to be in Bakery No. 9, or why I have it . . .'

Zam passed the runcible spoon to Phoebe. It began to glow in her hands.

'I think it can tell me where it came from,' she said. 'At the heart of the Forever Tree, an old lady has a tree-root workshop . . .'

And Phoebe told Zam the story of how the magical objects had been made especially for them and delivered by the bears.

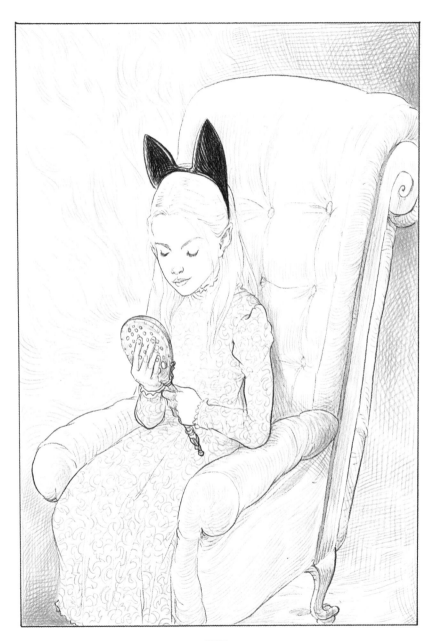

23

BATHSHEBA'S WISH

Bathsheba looked at the cello the girl had dropped when she fell between the boulders. Then she looked at the sword in her hand. Both the cello and the handle of her worpal sword were glowing. This must be the same tree magic the bears in her dream had talked about. She had been so sure the girl with the cello had been a professional princess, but she'd been wrong.

Just then, the soft, beguiling sound of flute music floated past Bathsheba, carried on the gentle breeze. She recognized it immediately. No, no, no. Not again!

Leaving the cello behind, she ran towards the sound. There in the distance, right on the edge of the Great Wood, sitting under a tree, was Euphemia Goldencurls playing her flute. She was never going to give up!

As Bathsheba quickened her pace, she saw the grey giant emerge from the Tumbledowns, his great face creased into an enchanted smile, his eyelids heavy. Bathsheba could see clearly that the flute was mesmerizing him, drawing the giant into the trap. Sure enough, as he reached Euphemia, there was the whirr of harpoons being fired from the cover of the trees, and then a sickening thud as they hit home.

The chains went taut, as they had last time, and the giant-slayers' wagon came bursting into view with the armoured giant-slayers clinging on for dear life.

Bathsheba was too far away to help him, so she changed direction and made for the treeline. The giant was now careering through the forest directly towards her. Bathsheba still had a chance to intercept the wagon but it wasn't going to be easy. She wished with all her might, 'Cut the chain . . . Cloud horse, cloud horse, far from view, make this— URGGHH!'

The giant thundered past, knocking Bathsheba to

one side, and sending her crashing into a tree trunk before she fell to the forest floor.

In the blackness, Bathsheba felt warmth on her cheek, then something soft nuzzling her face. She opened her eyes slowly and tried to focus. She was looking up at a velvet muzzle. Above it, two blue eyes with long lashes were staring back at her, and she could see a shock of cloud-white hair above them. It was a horse. It lowered its muzzle and nudged her gently under the chin, encouraging her to stand up.

As Bathsheba got to her feet, she saw that the horse was holding the handle of her worpal sword in its mouth and seemed to be looking at her expectantly. She took the sword.

'Thank you,' she said, then stepped back with a gasp as two enormous white feathered wings spread out on either side of the horse. It lowered its head, snorted softly, and pawed the ground with one hoof.

'You're . . . You're . . . A cloud horse,' she whispered, astonished. 'You're real and . . .'

The horse snorted again and pawed the ground insistently.

'Do you mean I can ride you?' asked Bathsheba. The cloud horse nodded.

Carefully, Bathsheba, heart beating fast, stepped round to the side of the horse and climbed up on to its back, between the magnificent outstretched wings. She reached forward, clutching its mane with one hand, and instantly the horse began to beat powerful wings. In moments, they were soaring up out of the dappled light of the forest floor and up into the clear blue sky.

Bathsheba looked down. She could hardly believe it. She was flying on a cloud horse; a real cloud horse. Below them was the jagged path through the forest made by the wounded giant. The cloud horse had seen it too, for it swerved down through the air

in a wide arc and followed the trail of splintered and fallen trees.

There, up ahead, was the giant-slayers' wagon being pulled by the harpooned giant. Euphemia was brandishing her worpal sword, while behind her, Tam and Shanter hurled spiked weights at the back of the increasingly tired giant.

The cloud horse swooped down even lower. Bathsheba reached out, and with the tip of her worpal sword, she knocked Tam and Shanter's helmets off and swept the wig right off the astonished Euphemia's head.

The cloud horse flew back up into the air and turned, flying directly towards the oncoming giant-slayers' wagon, allowing Bathsheba to slice through the harpoon chains, making the wagon lurch off the path and hit a tree.

The giant stumbled to a halt, breathing heavily, his hands on his haunches as he turned slowly round and glared at the upturned wagon and the

giant-slayers
sprawled on the
ground beside
it. With a
grimace, the giant
reached behind his back and
pulled out a handful
of harpoons. He
threw them to
the ground in
disgust, as the
terrified giant-
slayers leaped to
their feet, turned
tail and ran.

The cloud
horse swooped
down, beating its
wings slowly as it
hovered just above the forest floor.

Bathsheba slipped off its back and on to the ground.

'Thank you,' she said, stroking its flank. 'That was amazing.'

The cloud horse snorted, tossing its head, and with a steady beat of its wings, it rose back into the air and flew off across the treetops.

Bathsheba watched it go. She felt exhilarated. A cloud horse had answered her wish! Euphemia and her nasty crew had been taught a lesson they'd never forget. She stood for a moment, until the cloud horse disappeared from sight, then she became aware of heavy breathing. She looked up at the giant, who was still catching his breath. Sheathing her worpal sword, she broke into a huge smile. She reached into her tunic, and took out her notebook and pencil.

'No, don't tell me,' she said. 'Your name is Budlee Bristletoe.'

'How did you know?' asked the giant, astonished.

'I study giants,' said Bathsheba, settling herself

on the upturned wagon and turning to a fresh page in her notebook. 'Now, what I really want to know is why, when you must realize it's a trap, you still can't resist the sound of music?'

Budlee Bristletoe straightened up and then stroked his chin thoughtfully.

'It's not just any music,' he said. 'It's the music that comes from that.' He pointed to something half hidden in the undergrowth.

Bathsheba looked down. There, beside the wagon, was Euphemia's flute, glowing brightly. At Bathsheba's side, her worpal sword, she realized, was glowing equally brightly.

Bathsheba smiled. 'It must be tree magic,' she said.

'I can be clumsy,' admitted Budlee Bristletoe, lying on his back and looking up at the sky though the forest canopy. 'I never meant to knock down those tree houses. I just didn't see them in time . . .'

'Was that how the trouble started?' asked Bathsheba.

'I suppose so,' said Budlee. He twiddled the ends of his moss-covered neckerchief with his enormous spatula-like fingers. 'And the shouting didn't help.'

'The townsfolk shouted at you?' said Bathsheba sympathetically.

'No, I did the shouting. It's what we giants do when we're scared. But now I think about it, I suppose it could be a little frightening for small people . . .' Budlee continued with a frown.

'You might try to work on the shouting,' said Bathsheba. 'And on staying away from Beam.'

'I've tried,' said Budlee. 'But sometimes they play music in the town square, and it always sounds so exciting and full of life. I've told myself lots of times that I would just listen quietly from a distance, but before I knew it, I'd find myself dancing, which is when—'

'The tree houses got knocked down,' said Bathsheba.

'Yes – and the trouble started,' agreed Budlee Bristletoe. 'Now the Great Wood isn't safe for giants any more.'

'Well, it's not your fault,' said Bathsheba, closing her notebook and getting to her feet. 'I just wish the townsfolk could understand that.'

Budlee carefully put the wagon the right way up, and Bathsheba slipped the flute into her backpack. They began to walk back towards the Tumbledowns, with Budlee pulling the wagon behind him.

'That flying horse was amazing,' said Budlee. 'Where did you find it?'

'It *was* amazing,' agreed Bathsheba. 'But I didn't find it. It found me . . . I made a wish, and there it was. I think it might have something to do with tree magic too.'

'The old parts of the Great Wood are full of tree magic,' said Budlee as they stepped out from the forest and into the Tumbledowns. 'But the small people make machines to chop the forest down. If there's no forest, the tree magic will all be gone.'

'Machines?' asked Bathsheba. But before Budlee could reply, another voice interrupted them.

'Tin men,' said a girl standing on a boulder, looking down at them. She was holding the cello.

'You must be Bathsheba Greengrass from Beam,' said the girl, who seemed to be enjoying Bathsheba's look of surprise. 'My cello has been telling me all about you. Thank you for looking after her. My name's Phoebe Limetree. I'm from Nightingale.'

'And I'm Zam Zephyr,' said a boy, stepping out from behind the boulder next to Phoebe. 'From Troutwine.'

Bathsheba's eyes widened. Giants were emerging

from all around, in robes of matted moss, shawls of bark, and gowns of woven glade-grass. Grizell Barkfire appeared and, sweeping back her mushroom-flecked hair, gave Bathsheba a wide, gap-toothed smile.

'We thought the giant-slayers had finally got Budlee.' She beamed down at Bathsheba. 'But then you went chasing after them into the forest to save him. And now here you both are!'

The delicious smell of freshly baked bread floated past on the breeze, and Bathsheba saw that the giants were holding baskets containing large loaves.

She hopped over to join Zam and Phoebe,

while the giants collected in small groups of twos and threes and ate their bread.

'I met a cloud horse,' said Bathsheba excitedly. 'A real one! I made a wish and there it was. It let me fly on its back, and we defeated the giant-slayers together before it flew away!'

'It's true,' said Budlee, who was sitting nearby, his mouth full of bread. 'Bathsheba and the cloud horse saved my life.'

Zam and Phoebe exchanged looks.

'You made a wish? Interesting . . .' said Phoebe.

'Come down to the cavern kitchen,' said Zam. 'And tell us all about it.'

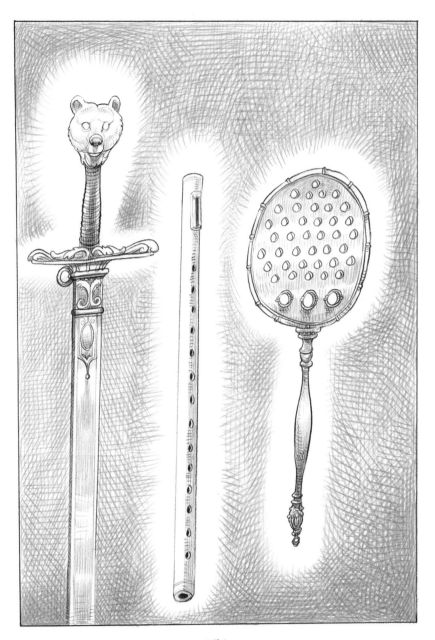

254

24

TOMORROW

Bathsheba Greengrass, Phoebe Limetree and Zam Zephyr sat at the large wooden table in the cavern kitchen. Phoebe was holding her cello, playing a soft, lilting song that echoed beautifully around the rocky walls. Zam leaned forward and carefully straightened the worpal sword, which Bathsheba had just placed on the table next to his runcible spoon.

Bathsheba reached into her backpack and handed Euphemia's flute to Zam. He put it neatly next to the sword and spoon. They all glowed, bathing the three children in a golden light.

'So we have this tree magic,' said Zam. 'But what do we do with it? Maybe we could help each other.'

'But how? The old lady made these things from Forever wood for a reason,' said Phoebe, 'and sent the lumberers to leave them for us to find. She

wants us to use them, doesn't she, cello?'

'I'm sure she does,' said the cello. 'But don't ask me how, I'm just a musical instrument.'

'You're much more to me than that,' said Phoebe, continuing to play. The cello chuckled, delighted.

'Let's think. The flute belonged to the Pied Piper,' said Zam. 'Bocklin told me all about it. One of the rats took it when the Piper was distracted. He was in love with the Duchess and neglecting the rats, who were developing bad habits. The rat lost it . . .'

'Lost it, or it was stolen, if I know Euphemia Goldencurls,' said Bathsheba. 'Which only goes to show, tree magic in the wrong hands can cause a lot of harm. One thing is certain,' she added. 'This worpal sword is not meant for giant slaying . . .'

'But it is very sharp,' said Zam, reaching out thoughtfully and touching the carved wooden handle. 'And you are so good with it, Bathsheba . . .' He paused, an idea starting to form. 'You cut the chains of a giant-slayer's wagon, so tent poles and guy ropes at a Troutwine tea ball wouldn't be a problem?'

'And the music from the flute,' added Bathsheba. 'It charmed the giants for Euphemia, but imagine what effect your beautiful cello music could have on the townsfolk of Beam, Phoebe?'

Phoebe smiled and turned excitedly to Zam. 'And you made your amazing gingerbread people with this spoon,' she told him. 'I think you could teach that Clockmaker a thing or two at the next awful Nightingale parade, Zam.'

'The next one is tomorrow, isn't it, Phoebe?' asked the cello.

'And it's also market day in Beam. The whole town will be there,' said Bathsheba.

'Bocklin's taken a batch of my pastries for the Grand Duchess's Tea Ball,' said Zam excitedly. 'He told me it had been rearranged after the last one was cancelled – and that's tomorrow too!'

The music from the cello rose and fell as the children's plan began to fall into place.

As the dawn rose over the Tumbledowns, three figures climbed from between the boulders and straightened up. Shielding their eyes, they looked up at the pink-tinged clouds, lit up from the sunrise, and made their wishes.

'Stop the Clockmaker and the tin men,' said Phoebe Limetree.

'Save the giants from Euphemia and the giant-slayers,' said Bathsheba Greengrass.

'Free Balthazar and stop King Rat,' said Zam Zephyr.

'Cloud horse, cloud horse, far from view . . .' The three children linked arms and spoke as one. 'Make this wish of mine come true.'

Just then, coming from above, there was the sound of beating wings.

'They're here,' said the cello.

25

THE CLOUD HORSES

Phoebe clutched her cello case in one hand and the mane of the cloud horse in the other. The cloud horse, its magnificent wings spread wide, soared high on the wind currents over the Great Wood. Far below, the treetops blurred into a rippling green carpet as it beat its wings and increased speed.

Before climbing up on to its back, Phoebe had looked into the horse's clear blue eyes and stroked its velvety grey muzzle. It was as if they'd known each other all their lives. The cloud horse seemed to understand her.

As it had lowered its head and nuzzled her, Phoebe had felt a warm feeling flood through her body. This cloud horse was *her* cloud horse – it would protect her, and she knew she could trust it.

As she'd climbed up on to the horse's back, she'd felt her spirits lift. Then, as the mighty wings began to beat, and they rose – girl and horse – up into the sky, Phoebe's heart began to beat fast, and she felt a wave of exhilaration engulf her. She leaned forward until her cheek was resting against the cloud horse's neck and whispered into its ear, 'Take me to Beam.'

Bathsheba threw back her head
and let out a great whoop of joy.

She felt as if she would burst if she didn't let it out. The cloud horse, *her* cloud horse, the same one who had defeated the giant-slayers with her, steadily beat its wings as they flew over the Tumbledowns and towards the distant smudge that was the Grey Hills. Beyond that were the twin peaks of Troutwine, not yet in view, but vivid in Bathsheba's imagination.

She reached down and felt the handle of the worpal sword reassuringly at her side. The cloud horse trembled beneath her, and Bathsheba knew it shared her excitement and her nervousness. They had their tree-magic gifts, which had been carefully left for each of them to find and use when the time came. And now that time had come.

Bathsheba checked the straps on her backpack and then peered at the horizon. Was that the glint of tall spires she could see? The cloud horse continued the steady beat of its wings, and they flew on, rising through the grey clouds into a bright blue sky.

Zam sat forward on his cloud horse's back. It seemed to be the youngest of the three extraordinary creatures that had landed on the boulders above the cavern kitchen. But as soon as their eyes had met, Zam knew that this was *his* cloud horse. They had greeted each other shyly at first, but as Zam had patted the cloud horse's neck, then reached into his pocket and offered a small piece of cinnamon bun, they seemed to bond.

The previous evening Zam had set to work immediately in the kitchen with his runcible spoon. It was as if every gingerbread person he'd baked so far had been a preparation for this, and Zam was ready for the challenge. The sugar and the spices of the flavour library had to be calibrated and mixed in just the right way if he was to achieve the effect that was needed.

Each of them had their gifts of tree magic, and now they needed to use them. Zam patted the neck of his cloud horse as they flew over the South River Falls

and on towards the great city of Nightingale. The three of them had been chosen by the old woman of the Great Wood. Now it was up to them to become guardians of magic – the Tumbledowners.

26

Sawdust, Cake and Menaces

The Clockmaker strode across the hall of a hundred clocks, the heels of his slippers click-clacking on the polished marble floor. The carved wooden cases of the clocks sighed and whispered, while from behind the glass panels, pendulums swayed, cog wheels ticked and tocked, and springs whirred. The faces of the clocks looked down at the Clockmaker from the black sockets of their winding keyholes, the spikey clock hands moving slowly across their features. The Clockmaker stopped in the middle of the hall and spread his arms wide.

'You are all my children,' he said, as he always did the minute before the clocks struck twelve.

As the hour struck, the hall filled with chimes, a hundred of them, each different in tone and pitch, striking twelve times. The Clockmaker knew them all. His clocks had taught him everything, and now the children of the hundred clocks, with their tin bodies and arms and legs, were gathering outside in Clocktower Square for the Nightingale Parade.

The Tin Man Timber Company had been a great success. With his clockwork army, the Clockmaker had been able to dominate Nightingale and the Five Towns. And that was only the beginning. The trees of the Great Wood were being harvested, the timber mills had never been busier, the furniture makers, palace builders, riverwrights and wagon makers were all working to capacity, and any wood left over was burned. The furnaces, stoves and hearths blazed. The tang of woodsmoke flavoured the air. The Clockmaker had made Nightingale tick; now it was time to tinker with the workings of Troutwine.

The Grand Duchess was a fool, and that piper of hers was a hollowed-out wreck. The rats were the ones who called the shots. They hated tree magic because they feared it. The Clockmaker didn't fear it;

he wanted to control it. With Troutwine in his grip, he would grow even stronger. Then he would deal with the lumberers once and for all, take the most ancient trees for himself, and turn them to sawdust. Precious sawdust!

The hall of a hundred clocks fell silent as the sounds of the twelfth chime faded. Then the air filled with the whirring of wings, and in through the high

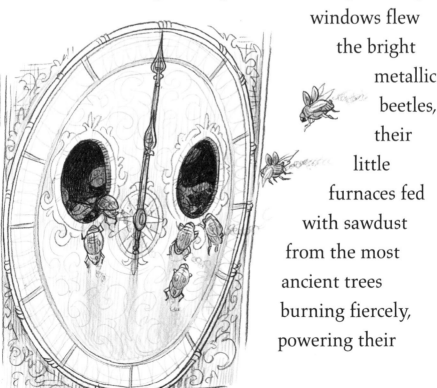

windows flew the bright metallic beetles, their little furnaces fed with sawdust from the most ancient trees burning fiercely, powering their metallic wings and glowing eyes. The Clockmaker looked on with satisfaction as, one by one, the beetles settled on the clock faces, then scuttled inside their keyhole eyes. The tin men outside were fully wound. It was time for the Nightingale Parade to begin . . .

King Tiberius-Tiberius pushed away a honey-glazed almond croissant and belched, his whiskers quivering. On either side of him, his rat attendants stepped forward to loosen his embroidered waistcoat and gently massage his distended tummy. King Tiberius-Tiberius pushed them away, reached for a tea cup, and began to slurp its contents down noisily. The Grand Duchess and her ladies-in-waiting watched, appalled.

The League of Rats had been tolerated in Troutwine ever since their first appearance. The handsome young Pied Piper had charmed the court with his clever performing rodents in their neat little waistcoats. They had danced elegantly for the fine ladies, and conjured gold coins from the pockets of the noble gentlemen. The Piper had also charmed the young Grand Duchess, it was said, for he and his flute had never been far from her side in those days. Now he was stooped with premature age and was rarely seen, and his flute was long gone.

The rats had long since abandoned him, taking to the sewers and increasing in size and numbers. Now the rats were as big as cats and they collected payment from every bakery in the city. The Grand Duchess just wanted a quiet life. She really didn't care what went on outside the palace gates as long as she was left out of it. Perhaps that awful Clockmaker could do what he'd promised and control the League of Rats, unlike her poor old Piper.

The Grand Duchess tutted as she rose from the chair with as much dignity as she could muster, and walked away from the Troutwine tea ball.

'Let them eat cake,' she muttered.

Euphemia combed out her second-best wig and pulled it on over her short raven-black hair. She picked up the sheaf of paper from her dressing table and checked her reflection in the mirror. She didn't look too bad, considering her latest little setback, she told herself.

'The best professional princess in the business,' she murmured approvingly, then frowned. 'But what business?'

She had been counting on returning to Beam in triumph with the head and possessions of the notorious wrecker of tree houses, Budlee Bristletoe. Then, in the town square, surrounded by cheering market-day crowds, she could have started to put in place her plans for Beam: an alliance with the King Rat, Tiberius-Tiberius of Troutwine, and the Clockmaker and tin men of Nightingale, in exchange for what she wanted. She would have been the new Grand Duchess of Troutwine in no time. The Society of Giant-Slayers, with Euphemia Goldencurls, professional princess, at their head, were more than a match for anyone. But things hadn't gone to plan. There was no slain giant to boast about. But Euphemia knew where to find some. They were hiding out in the Tumbledowns, not bothering anyone. Well, that was no use to her. She swept back her second-best golden locks, and cleared her throat, as she raised the sheaf of paper.

'People of Beam, the giant menace is real. I have seen it with my own eyes, and the Society of Giant-Slayers must unite to face this threat,' Euphemia read aloud with a flourish.

'Budlee Bristletoe is back. And this time, he is angry!'

276

27

GUARDIANS OF MAGIC

The cloud horse flew down low over the town square of Beam. The stallholders stepped away from their barrows of disapproving marrows and pale-looking pumpkins and shielded their eyes as they gazed up. The Society of Giant-Slayers, gathered around their wagons in front of the bandstand, bristled as they watched the flying horse swoop down to land.

The townsfolk of Beam chattered excitedly as they began to run towards the bandstand, pointing and shouting to one another. They clutched baskets half full of meagre vegetables grown in the undernourished fields cleared of forest on the edges of the town. The cloud horse landed beside the bandstand, and the crowd gave a collective gasp as it folded its magnificent wings and a small girl climbed down from its back clutching a cello case.

The girl settled herself on the edge of the bandstand and, taking a cello from the case, began to play.

Euphemia Goldencurls, at the head of a group of professional princesses, a sheaf of paper in her hand, was about to step forward and deliver her speech, but a look from the cloud horse made her fall back. She glanced over to the forest fringing the square in case there were dark-furred bears waiting to pounce, but she couldn't see anything.

The girl continued to play the most beautiful music anyone had ever heard. It was magical, but not in the mesmerizing way of the flute. Phoebe's talent to create music had a power all of its own.

Suddenly, from around the square, there were shouts of alarm as heads, then shoulders, began to appear out of the treetops. The trees on the edge of the town square swayed and shook as giants stepped out of the forest and stared down at the terrified townsfolk of Beam. There were at least eight of them, and the giant-slayers huddled together, their armour rattling and harpoons shaking as they trembled in fear. The tallest giant, with long, mushroom-flecked hair that reached to her ankles, leaned forward and picked up one of the giant-slayers' wagons.

Euphemia drew her worpal sword and sprang forward. 'Put that wagon down!' she commanded.

'Certainly,' said Grizell Barkfire, sweeping the contents of her apron into the wagon and placing it beside the bandstand as Phoebe continued to play.

The crowd gasped in surprise, and then in pleasure. The wagon was full of an astonishing array of mushrooms. As the giant-slayers looked on, open mouthed, the other giants picked up wagons, filled them with the contents of the forage bags and folded cloaks they were wearing, and placed them carefully around the bandstand as Phoebe played on. The townsfolk of Beam swept forward, brushing the Society of Giant-Slayers aside. Succulent forest fruits, glistening pine and chestnuts, wild honeycomb and strawberries filled the wagons to

overflowing, and the crowd helped themselves.

Tam raised a harpoon, only to have it snatched out of his hand and thrown to the ground by a woman with a basket full of mushrooms. Euphemia pulled off her wig and sheathed her worpal sword before disappearing into the crowd. The townspeople, swaying to the music and holding their overflowing baskets above their heads, had begun chanting, 'Long live the giants! Down with the giant-slayers!'

As the townspeople and the giants mingled, the chants turning to songs, Phoebe put away her cello, climbed on to her cloud horse's back, and slipped quietly away.

The cloud horse's wing tip grazed the top of the pavilion, and, reaching down, Bathsheba cut the guy ropes with a sweep of her worpal sword. The canvas collapsed on to Tiberius-Tiberius and the carousing cake-splattered rats below. On the palace steps, the Grand Duchess and her ball guests watched in astonishment as the cloud horse soared up, over their heads and towards a high tower. It circled the tower several times before hovering with great circular beats of its wings in front of a tall window. Bathsheba took the flute from her backpack and reached out. A pale hand, gnarled and wrinkled, appeared at the window and took the flute from Bathsheba's outstretched hand, before she and the cloud horse flew away.

'I've missed you,' said a cracked voice.

Zam's cloud horse flew across the sky above Clocktower Square, casting a flickering shadow over the ranks of tin men marching below. The folk of Nightingale murmured as they stared up at the winged horse. From the balcony below the clocktower, the Clockmaker shook his fist in frustration.

'Destroy them!' he commanded.

In answer, from the hundred clocks behind him,

283

the metallic beetles emerged and gathered in a great whirring swarm. Like an ominous glittering cloud, the beetles flew out of the high window and, eyes glowing, set off after the cloud horse and rider.

Zam glanced over his shoulder and realized that the time had come to play his part. He had baked hundreds of gingerbread butterflies with the runcible spoon and now the plan was to release them over Nightingale.

He had mixed the ingredients and baked them as carefully as he could. But would they work? Zam felt a nagging doubt. What if he'd made a mistake? What if he let everyone down? He thought of Phoebe and Bathsheba, and reached out and touched the cloud horse's neck. He *could* do this. *They* could do this.

Zam pulled on the string securing the bundle behind him, and the cloth unfolded. Small gingerbread butterflies flapped their spiced wings, which had been delicately cut out and baked, and took to the air.

The cloud horse circled over the square as the tin men marched to and fro in a dazzling, ever-changing kaleidoscope . . .

28

THE PIPER & THE CLOCKMAKER

The Piper stepped out from the tower and walked down the palace steps. His clothes were a faded patchwork of different shades of white, his long sleeves frayed, the peaked hat crumpled and adorned with a white skeletal feather. He held the glowing flute to his lips and played.

The scritch-scratching of claws on stone could be heard, and as the Piper walked through the palace gardens and through the gates, a throng of rats scampered on all fours around his heels. He walked slowly and steadily, pausing only to tip his hat to the tearful Grand Duchess gazing after him from the steps, surrounded by her astonished courtiers and the palace guards, who looked relieved.

The Piper played as he walked through the streets of Troutwine, sewer grilles popping up in his wake as

mesmerized rats scrambled after him, their whiskers quivering. Waistcoats, catapults, spikes and chains were tossed aside as the rats seemed to shrink in size and return to their sleek sinuous selves. The Piper's eyes wrinkled in happiness as they left Troutwine and headed south towards the Tumbledowns. All over the city, people gathered to collect the discarded objects and marvel at the rats' departure. Few noticed the cats gathered on rooftops, hats pulled down low and shoulders hunched as they conversed in low voices.

'Do you think the elves will be returning?'

'Too early to say . . .'

Zam looked back and felt a shiver of alarm run through him. The copper-coloured beetles were breaking from the swarm and hunting down the fluttering gingerbread butterflies that his runcible spoon had brought to life. The beautiful flying biscuits were being nibbled to bits by hundreds of glowing-eyed beetles. The butterflies crumbled under attack and splintered into crumbs, each one swallowed by the greedy mechanical insects. But nothing happened.

The plan hadn't worked. Zam turned away and buried his face in the cloud horse's mane. Below, the steady *tramp, tramp, tramp* of the marching tin men echoed round Clocktower Square.

From the balcony, the Clockmaker raised his fist. 'Now, my beetles, keepers of my clocks, will bring you and your horse back down to earth,' he promised.

As the cloud horse flew back round the square, Zam looked up and braced himself for the beetles to attack. The swarm finished the last of the gingerbread butterflies and gathered in an ominous cloud, then sped towards him.

Suddenly, bright flashes, like bolts of lightning, spread through the swarm, followed by a *pop-pop-pop* sound as the beetles began to explode.

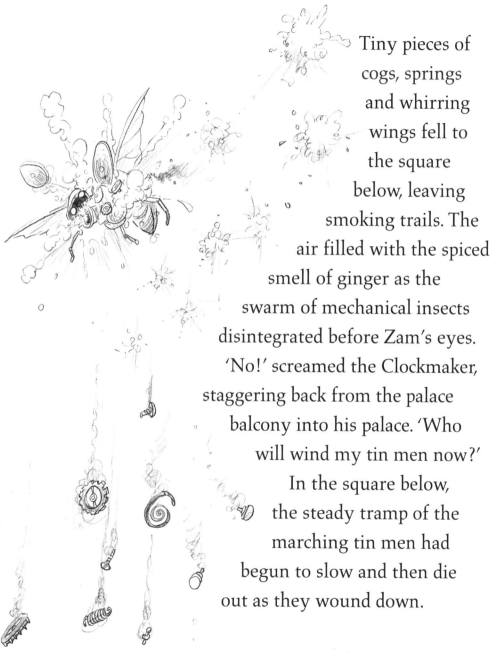

Tiny pieces of
cogs, springs
and whirring
wings fell to
the square
below, leaving
smoking trails. The
air filled with the spiced
smell of ginger as the
swarm of mechanical insects
disintegrated before Zam's eyes.
'No!' screamed the Clockmaker,
staggering back from the palace
balcony into his palace. 'Who
will wind my tin men now?'
In the square below,
the steady tramp of the
marching tin men had
begun to slow and then die
out as they wound down.

The crowd began to
murmur, and then
break through the
cordon ropes that
contained them,
as the tin men
ground to a halt.
With no beetles
to wind them
up, the tin men
were stationary
targets, and
the jubilant crowd seized the
axes from the frozen mechanical
figures and started to chop them
up. The sounds of clanging and
the flash of sparks followed
Zam as his cloud horse rose
high in the air and flew them
both towards the north.

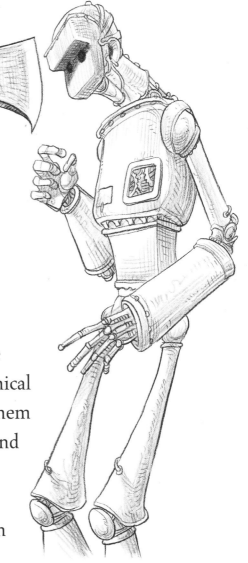

29

SEE YOU IN THE TUMBLEDOWNS

It was a small cart pulled by a particularly
ill-tempered gruff but it was all the Clockmaker
could find at such short notice. Not surprising really,
considering how it had ended, he thought bitterly.
What with his trunk of tools and his favourite clock,
there was barely enough space in the cart for him,
let alone his passenger.

'Careful with those elbows!' Euphemia
Goldencurls complained as they went over the latest
of a series of bumps in the forest track.

'The bottom has fallen out of the giant-slaying
business,' she complained, not for the first time. 'So
what are we going to do now?'

'We?' said the Clockmaker, raising an eyebrow
disdainfully.

'Yes, we,' insisted Euphemia, tossing aside the

golden wig and raking her fingers through her short black hair. 'And you can call me Euphemia Ravenhair from now on. Like it or not, you've got a sidekick.'

The Clockmaker attempted a thin smile. This Beamish girl had her faults but she was persistent, and he admired that.

'Well, Euphemia . . . Ravenhair,' he said, reaching out a protecting arm to steady the clock. 'What we do next rather depends on him.' He nodded at the driver of the cart, a large cat in expensive-looking boots. 'And the elves, of course.'

Zam circled the square on the back of his cloud horse. Below, the last of the tin men were being loaded on to wagons, ready to be taken back to the foundry. The brass bands of Nightingale were going to be making a spectacular comeback when the metal was recycled. In the distance, another

cloud horse had come into view over the farmlands on the other side of the river, and Zam flew towards it.

Phoebe waved to Zam, her cello in its case, securely strapped to her back as the cloud horse swooped past. A few moments later, Bathsheba's cloud horse appeared, diving down through the clouds to join them.

'So we did it!' she called out, waving her worpal sword triumphantly. 'The Piper has his rats back and the Grand Duchess is waiting to see you, Zam.'

'And the giants are waiting to see you,' Phoebe called to Bathsheba, as she flew past. 'They were having a party with the townsfolk when I left, and there was no sign of Euphemia.'

'You'll find the cat orchestra tuning up in Clocktower Square,' Zam told Phoebe, as the cloud horses fell into formation. 'They want you to play a midnight concert with them as loudly as you can. They said you'd understand.'

The cloud horses on either side swooped to
the right and left, and Zam's carried straight on.
'See you in the Tumbledowns,' he called over his
shoulder to Phoebe and Bathsheba.

30
Watching Over Us

'Are you sure you won't change your mind?' asked
Balthazar Boabab. 'After all, the League of Rats has
gone, and Bakery No. 9 is open for business again,
thanks to you. How did you get the Grand Duchess
to pardon me?'

Zam smiled. 'I took her for a ride on my cloud
horse. Just around the Troutwine crags, and she was
so delighted, she asked what she could do for me in
return.'

Zam shook Balthazar's hand. 'Thank you for the
job offer, but I have a bakery of my own now.' he
explained.

'In the Tumbledowns,' said Balthazar Boabab
thoughtfully. 'A strange part of the world . . . But if
you change your mind, you'll always have a job here
with me.'

302

'We won't change our minds,' said Langdale the goat boy. 'I'm looking forward to seeing the Tumbledowns for myself. Now where's that cloud horse of yours?' he added, looking out of the window of Bakery No. 9.

'He comes when I need him,' said Zam. 'That's all I know. Now pick up your bags, Langdale – there is a water badger I want you to meet.'

'I'm going to miss you, Phoebe, my dear,' said Madame Arpeggio, wiping away a tear. 'And so will the cat orchestra.' They were standing on the steps of Fairweather House, and behind them, the cats waved and miaowed their goodbyes.

'Do come back and visit us soon,' said Madame Arpeggio, stroking the music case Phoebe was holding. 'Both of you.'

'We will,' said Phoebe, turning reluctantly to go.

'Is it true that you have a flying horse that takes

you everywhere, just like that boy in Clocktower Square?' asked Madame Arpeggio.

'Only when I really need her,' said Phoebe with a smile. 'It's a gruff cart to Spindle Falls for me, and then I'm meeting a water badger and some friends . . .'

'Beam has certainly changed since your friends paid us a visit,' said Miss Mahalia. 'The Society of Giant-Slayers has been run out of town, but they're still out there somewhere, so you take care.'

'I will,' said Bathsheba, gazing up at the Boot House Orphanage. 'And I'll come back to see you on market days,' she added with a smile.

'With Grizell Barkfire and Budlee Bristletoe?' asked Miss Mahalia, eyes twinkling. 'The market's really something to look forward to, now the giants are bringing us the gifts of the forest.'

Bathsheba gazed up at the sky.

'Are you expecting a flying horse to swoop down

and carry you away?' Miss Mahalia asked, before enveloping Bathsheba in a great big hug.

'She'll come when I need her,' said Bathsheba. 'It's what cloud horses do.'

She smiled as she hugged Miss Mahalia and then stepped back. 'They watch over you.'

The cloud horses circled high in the sky above the Forever Tree, then as the dawn broke, they spread their wings and followed the others into the distant cloud pastures.

The covered wagon belonging to the Ursine Ballet Troupe of the West drew up outside the workshop in the roots of the Forever Tree. The old woman was waiting. 'Let's have some porridge,' she said to the bears.

They went inside and sat at a workbench while the old woman served up breakfast. She sat down with the three bears and picked up a spoon. The porridge wasn't too hot, it wasn't too cold . . . It was just right.